THE FINAL GIRL

A. S. FRENCH

NEONOIR BOOKS

Writing as Andrew. S. French

Science Fiction

The Time Traveller's Murder

The Mercy Sleep

Bodies

The Arcane Supernatural Thriller Series

Book one: The Arcane

Book two: The Arcane Identity

Book three: The Arcane Quest

Book four: The Arcane Ultimatum

The Ella Finn Fantasy Novella Series

Ella and the Elementals

Ella and the Multiverse

Ella and the Monsters

Ella and the Dreamers

Supernatural Short Stories

Dead Souls

The Shadow

Go to www.andrewsfrench.com for more information.

1 JULIA

The rain vanished as the man dropped his daughter off the bridge.

Julia clutched at the air, her neck twisted up to see her parents smiling at her. It was the last thing she saw before she hit the water. The river punched its way through her lips, rushed into her mouth and possessed her lungs. She flailed her arms and legs, searching for stability, dragged further into the darkness. The cold bit at her flesh as she grabbed for her throat, her eyes wide as gravity drew her further down.

As invisible fingers wrapped themselves around her heart, a hand reached down and pulled her out of the river. Her eyes flickered open to see her father drag her into the mud. Julia's mother was with him, frowning at her daughter. Julia rolled onto her side and coughed up water, struggling to breathe through the throbbing of her lungs.

'This is what happens when you're a bad girl, Julia.'

She gazed into her mother's eyes and didn't recognise the person there.

'Get up and into the car,' her father said.

The rain came once more as she stood, mud clinging to her fingers as insects crawled over her feet. She limped to the car as pain surged through her. Nobody talked all the way back to the compound.

From then on, she rarely spoke around other people.

It was six months later when her parents hurt her again.

'Put this on,' her mother said as she handed Julia the blindfold. 'Then you'll get your presents.'

It was Julia's tenth birthday, but she didn't celebrate. Instead, they locked her in a cramped cupboard for eight hours, telling her not to remove the blindfold or the monsters would hurt her.

But the monsters had already got her.

When she took the blindfold off, she saw a yellow-eyed rat gazing at her in the gloom as it sat on top of her old doll's house.

It was hard for her to remember where they lived then, but she thought it was somewhere north. Her family moved around a lot after that: Newcastle, Middlesbrough, Bradford, Sheffield, Nottingham, Shrewsbury, Ipswich, Kings Lynn, even a few weeks in Padstow, where she enjoyed rare trips to the sea. Some places they stayed in were flats – tiny, unclean dwellings – but others were on farms or in large compounds with other families.

Julia was born into a vast family – more than a hundred adults and fifty-two children, of which she was the fifty-second. As she got older, it grew in size and was called The Community – a family not based on blood, but shared beliefs.

Everything she did was within The Community – all the children were home-schooled, and members of her extended family were qualified doctors and nurses, so nobody had to go outside for medical help unless it was an emergency. That was how the nurse saw the bruises on her body and Julia told her what had been happening in the family home. And the events on the bridge.

There was a trial – she didn't know it was called that at the time – and she remembered watching her mother and father answering questions about their daughter. They blamed her for their actions – she was a bad girl, sick in the head and evil. Julia never understood why they said those things about her.

Her parents were banished from The Community. It didn't matter to her as she had lots of other mums and dads to look after her. And they never hit her or locked her in a cupboard.

Or dropped her off a bridge.

When they'd left, Julia developed an interest in singing and music, learning to play the guitar and write lyrics. She was thirteen then, and it was the start of her new life, a much better one than she'd had with the birth parents. She soon forgot their names and couldn't remember them now, many years later.

Around this time, the elders of The Community introduced Julia to their leader. His name was Charles Wood, and he gave her the first present of her new life. She was sitting with a group of younger children when he approached them. His eyes mesmerised her, shimmering with different colours – one blue, the other green. He had an acoustic guitar in his hands.

'This is for you,' he said.

She took it from him, the smile warming her face. 'Thank you.'

He ran a finger through her hair. 'Now you can sing to the little ones.'

So she did. The songs were all her own since The

Community restricted access to entertainment in the outside world. From that moment on, her life improved – until death came calling.

Julia was living on a farm near St Albans. It was months after her birth parents' banishment, and she was staying in a communal room with other kids her age. One of her tasks was to milk the cows. The bucket chilled her fingers as she stepped into the barn with the morning's songs still inside her head, the wind caressing her cheeks. She was humming a tune about flowers when she saw the body.

She couldn't move, her legs frozen to the ground as the cows peered at her. Then she dropped the bucket, so it rolled over the dirt and stopped at the dead man. He was lying on his back, staring at her; his neck twisted to the side as blood seeped out of him and turned the grass red.

His name was Martin, one of the older men who worked the crops for The Community. Julia didn't scream. Once you've been thrown from a bridge and tortured by your parents, it takes a lot to shock you. So instead, she stepped towards him, holding her breath as the aroma of fresh blood oozed into her head. Her knees creaked as she bent down, placing a hand on his to see if he was alive. His skin chilled hers, making the hairs on the back of her neck stand up.

She didn't know how long she stayed there, but eventually, she left to get an elder.

The police arrived an hour later. A kind woman asked Julia questions about Martin, who she hardly knew. However, the other officers were not so friendly, eyeing her and all the other members of The Community with suspicion.

It took a long time for them to complete their investigation, at one point accusing Charles Wood of mistreating his flock. That was their word – flock – with Julia only realising later it was meant as an insult because the police saw her and the others as lambs manipulated by Wood. Eventually, Martin's death was classed as an accident.

Julia and some of the other children weren't so sure. There had been rumours of a falling out between the elders, with Martin at the centre of the disagreement. That's when one of the older kids, Grace, brought the Ouija out.

'There's life after death,' she told Julia and the others, 'and we can communicate with them. We'll talk to Martin and find out what happened to him.'

Julia was scared, but that fear soon turned into curiosity. The Ouija board was hand-carved, the woodgrain beautifully polished, the pointer covered in purple velvet. Only Grace could ask questions; Julia's eyes were glued to the pointer as it slid over the surface, moving slowly at first before picking up speed, with the low swish of felt on wood the only sound.

Julia held her breath as Grace spelt out the first question.

What happened to Martin?

There were six of them around the board, all tense as they waited.

He was murdered.

A collective gasp.

Who killed him?

A pause that lasted an eternity.

Julia.

They pulled their fingers away, their eyes peering into Julia.

'Why did you kill Martin?' Grace said to her.

She denied it, but Julia saw the fear in them, in those kids she thought were her friends. None of them trusted her after that. Then, days later, she realised Grace had moved the pointer between the letters. But it was too late then. All the others were wary of her.

It was a lesson learned for Julia, an important one that would shape the rest of her future and lead to her changing her name.

But there were other things to learn before that.

2 ASTRID'S FAMILY

Astrid took a deep breath and readied to knock on the door, carrying a bag containing the presents she'd brought back from America for her niece. She'd waited a week to get in touch, expecting something from Courtney which she hadn't given to her in over thirty years – concern for her younger sister.

She raised her hand, intrigued to see how calm her fingers were while every bone, muscle and sinew trembled like a roller-coaster. Through their childhood, her sister's indifference and malice had grown to a point where Astrid held it on the same level as her father's violence towards her. She'd never forgiven Courtney for her behaviour, but over the past year, Astrid had reduced her hatred for her sister so she could have a relationship with her niece, Olivia.

But Courtney hadn't made it easy – not that Astrid expected her to – and Astrid's extended trip to America had only allowed her sister to drive a bigger wedge between her and Olivia. Her only optimism came from the knowledge her niece had shown her nothing but love.

Yet here she was, doubting herself again as her brain

told her to bang on the door while her heart warned her of imminent disappointment. She puffed out her cheeks, sucked in cold air, and ignored her heart.

'There's no one home.'

The words surprised her so much, she nearly toppled over. Astrid steadied herself with a hand on the door, and a tiny splinter of wood pricked her skin.

'Fuck!'

Blood trickled into her palm as she turned to see the owner of that voice – an older woman, seventy or so, with small eyes and a narrow mouth that couldn't stop moving.

'That's shocking language, dear. Didn't your mother teach you any manners?'

Astrid sucked on her blood like a hungry vampire.

'She taught me how to smoke and drink; that was about it.'

And how to be a terrible parent. But I'm not a mother, only an aunt.

The woman stepped closer, her eyes shrinking inside her yellowed flesh as her wrinkled lips cracked a dark smile.

'You don't look like a drunk, but the good ones hide it well. My Charlie did.' She smelt like week-old potatoes. 'For thirty years, he'd go to work, and no one knew his dirty little secret. He never went to pubs or office parties – he'd come back here and drink enough to give him the courage to do what he'd always wanted to do.'

Astrid didn't ask what that was. 'You live next door?'

'All my life, lady. Aren't you going to ask what he did when full of drink?'

Astrid tightened her grip on the bag of presents. 'I can guess.'

The darkness sparkled in the old woman's eyes. 'Ah, are you one of those people who likes to hide from the truth of the world's depravity? Or perhaps you're the opposite: someone who has experienced the horrors of humanity and nothing shocks you anymore.'

Astrid didn't have the time or inclination to banter with the neighbour.

'Do you know where my sister and niece are?'

'Sister? You're Courtney's sister?' A cloud of gloom settled over the old woman's head. 'I don't have good news, lady.'

Astrid dropped the bag to the ground, her heart pumping so hard, she expected it to burst through her ribs.

'What do you mean?'

'They're always arguing, Courtney and that bloke of hers. It's so loud, it's impossible not to hear, even with a gap between our houses. And then there are the louder noises: the banging and the broken furniture.'

Astrid struggled to control her breathing. 'He's been hitting her?'

She shrugged. 'I never saw it, but, well, when you know, you know. I saw no evidence, saw no bruises.' Her laugh made the hairs stand up on the back of Astrid's neck. 'He's clever, that one, just like my Charlie.'

'You saw Olivia's father?'

The woman picked at a spot on her chin. 'No, but I could always hear the voices shouting at each other.' She poked at her ear. 'And I'm going deaf.'

'When was the last time you saw Courtney or Olivia?'

'At least two weeks. There was an almighty crash from the kitchen, and your sister stepped out of the back door. I watched her from my window – she was swearing at some-body, and there was a cut on her hand.'

Something old but not forgotten rose through Astrid, a tremulous shiver of anxiety originating from her childhood.

'Do you have a spare key to the house?'

The old woman shook her head. 'Sorry, lady.'

Astrid wasted no more time. She picked up the bag and went around the back, without saying goodbye to the neighbour. She'd never seen the garden before, but was unsurprised to find freshly cut grass. Astrid had always been messy as a kid, leaving dirty plates everywhere and dumping her clothes over every piece of furniture. It was just another thing Astrid did that attracted her mother's indifference and her father's anger.

But Courtney was the opposite, neat and tidy in everything she did. It made sharing a bedroom with her a nightmare. So discovering the rear of the house was cleaner than a hospital operating theatre wasn't a surprise. The small yellow and blue bike propped up against the fence separating the property from the field on the other side was the only thing out of place. The fence was as tall as Astrid, over six feet, so she had to perch on her toes to peer over it. There was nothing but long grass and trees as far as the horizon.

She turned and returned to the bike, putting her hand on the seat and wondering when was the last time Olivia had ridden it. As the image ran through her head, she got her phone and opened the Contacts. There were only two numbers on the list, and she hit the top one and waited for it to ring. It warbled for nearly a minute before switching to Courtney's voicemail. Astrid ended the call and stared at the back door, considering how she'd get inside without damaging a window.

Perhaps the nosey neighbour had a spare key after all. But, no, Courtney wouldn't do anything like that. She guarded her privacy too much to allow anyone else into her inner sanctum.

Breaking glass it was, then.

Astrid was bending to pick up a stone when she noticed something she hadn't seen since she was fourteen. It was pushed against the brick so tightly it would be impossible to see unless you knew it was there; or, like Astrid, discovered it by accident – a small metallic box. It was yellower and rustier than the last time she'd seen it: her final night in the Snow family home.

She hesitated, sliding her fingers across the top of the box as the metal rubbed against her skin. The surrounding dirt indicated it hadn't been moved for some time. When she got her nails underneath it and prised it loose, the damp bit into her flesh, and tiny insects scurried away. She lifted her body and the box, peering at it as if she was a teenager again and hearing her sister scream at her for touching it.

It was Courtney's necklace case.

It was too small to contain more than one jewellery item, so Courtney changed what was inside depending upon her current boyfriend. Most of them were thugs and hooligans, so she was never short of gifts teenagers couldn't afford.

The box rattled as Astrid shook it between her fingers, a smile creeping across her face as she opened it and grabbed the key. She slipped the dirty box into her jacket and the key into the lock. She had to wriggle it a few times before it turned. She removed the key and pushed her way in.

The kitchen was spotless. It was her first time in there since, on the few occasions Courtney had allowed her into the house, she'd never let Astrid out of the living room. Astrid headed there through the corridor, stepping inside to find it empty. She searched through the chest of drawers and the writing desk in the corner. There were a few bills in

Courtney's name, but there was nothing to identify where she and Olivia might be.

And there was no evidence of anybody else living in the house, no mention of Olivia's father.

But did Cortney live with him? Astrid had never met him or seen any photos of him or them as a family. Did he even exist? The neighbour said she'd heard raised voices and the sounds of violence, but she was hardly reliable. It might have been a loud TV making the noise.

Astrid considered that as she went upstairs. At the top, she saw two bedrooms and a bathroom. She stepped into the main bedroom. It was the smell that hit her first, that unmistakable aroma of burnt copper.

Blood. Not fresh, but not old.

She followed the odour, strode past the bed, and peered at the dark stain on the light carpet. Her knees creaked as she bent to get a closer look at the dried blood. She didn't touch it, wary of contaminating it with her DNA, but stared hard at it.

Two or three days at the most.

But whose blood was it?

Astrid resisted the urge to rush to Olivia's room, calming her throbbing heart. She went through every cupboard, wardrobe and drawer, careful not to leave fingerprints behind. Just like downstairs, there was no evidence of Courtney sharing the house with anyone apart from her daughter.

She stepped out and moved to the bathroom. Inside, she found towels, shampoo, toothpaste, two toothbrushes, and a range of shower products. She opened the cabinet, checking through the medication and seeing nothing unusual or suspicious. Then she took a deep breath and went to Olivia's room.

Colour leapt at Astrid from everywhere, from the patterned wallpaper full of animals to bedclothes stolen from a rainbow. The floor was dark wood, and it creaked as she stepped inside. Bright fluffy toys sat on the shelves and the bed: tall purple penguins nuzzled up to vibrant orange unicorns and grizzled green dragons.

She fell on the bed and gazed at the ceiling. Astrid ran her fingers over the cover and closed her eyes. The emotions that threatened to overwhelm her filled her with so much confusion, she thought she might be drowning. Why did she feel like this for someone else's child? Courtney was her sister, but there'd been no sisterly love between them; quite the opposite. So why did she care like this for her niece? It was a conundrum that had puzzled her from the start when she learned about Olivia's existence seven years ago. She did nothing about it for five years before giving in and assuming seeing the kid just once would rid her of those problematic emotions.

But that's not how it worked out; and seeing Olivia that first time, when the nanny brought her to the park, only strengthened her feelings.

The nanny.

She shot up from the bed. Did Courtney stop using a nanny after what happened last year? Astrid had visited the house twice before today, and there had been no sign of a nanny. But then again, there was no sign of the father.

The thought of him made her blood freeze, but it wasn't the image of Olivia's mysterious parent that turned her insides to ice; it was her own.

Could Astrid's father have something to do with Courtney and Olivia's disappearance?

Lawrence.

She hated thinking of him as her father. As far as he was

concerned, Lawrence only had one daughter – only one that mattered – and that was Courtney. From the day she was born, Astrid was an inconvenience to him until he realised inflicting pain on her made him happy. So she tried not to think of him at all.

Lawrence. Courtney had hinted he'd been in touch with her, had even met Olivia, but Astrid had seen no proof. He'd done his own disappearing act after his release from prison, but she could track him down if needed. It would be easy if she asked the Agency for help, but that would involve doing the two things she'd sworn never to do: return to the Agency and to him.

Lawrence.

No. There were other things she could do before reaching for the last resort. She slipped off the bed and went through Olivia's stuff, trying to keep her emotions in check as she handled her niece's clothes. She held the shoes for too long before checking the bookcase. It pleased her to see how many books the kid had, everything from Horrible Histories to Roald Dahl. She ran her fingers across the spines and remembered the bag of presents she'd left downstairs.

She sat back on the bed and opened the chest of drawers, finding socks and a notebook in the top one. Astrid flicked through the pages, reading her niece's words about her friends and being at school.

I shouldn't be looking at her private thoughts.

But maybe there would be something in there to tell her where Olivia and Courtney were. She spent two minutes spying on her niece's innermost feelings, finding only comments about school before stopping and closing the notebook.

Astrid returned to the drawer where she'd found the diary, ready to close it when she spotted a crumpled piece of paper. She grabbed it, rubbing her fingers over it before unfurling the paper. Even after all this time, she recognised her sister's handwriting – Courtney had always had a peculiar way of printing text, writing the letter V as if it was two fingers giving the age-old British insult.

VAN

GUARD

She stared at it for a long time, wondering if Courtney had needed to employ a security firm for protection.

And if so, protection from who?

From Olivia's mysterious father?

She slipped the paper into her pocket and returned to the bedside furniture.

Or perhaps it was protection from me? Olivia did nearly die because of me.

Astrid opened the second drawer, finding two photographs. The first was of Courtney and Olivia at the seaside, smiling together as they ate giant ice cream cones under a blistering sun, the resemblance between mother and daughter so unsettling, Astrid nearly dropped the photo on the carpet.

She gathered herself and peered at it. It seemed recent, perhaps taken when Astrid was in America. How had she not realised Olivia looked like a younger version of Courtney before? This sudden realisation shocked her system, but not as much as the other picture. She took it and lay on the bed again, holding the image up so it obscured the blank white space of the ceiling. That photograph made her feel as if she was the most important person in the world: Olivia grinned into the camera – Astrid knew the photo was from last year – as her small arms and tiny frame clung to her Aunt Astrid.

How could I have forgotten this moment?

She'd just returned Olivia to her mother after the two of them had survived a murderous attack by one of Astrid's former flames. She peered at their faces in the picture, remembering the relief she'd felt and the happiness Olivia projected. Courtney was apoplectic, of course, with every right, but Astrid didn't remember her sister taking this photo.

The father wasn't there then, either. So what did my sister tell me about that? Did she even mention him?

She focused on the photo and racked her brain for the memory of the night she'd put Olivia in danger. Astrid pushed aside the image of the park and the pain she'd felt from the gunshot wound in her shoulder, reaching back to that moment in this house.

Courtney must have taken the photo, and I didn't realise it. Yet here I am, staring straight into the camera lens.

Astrid lay there for an undetermined length of time before realising what she had to do. She got off the bed, closed the drawer, placed the two photos into her pocket, and went downstairs. She locked the back door and slipped the key into her sister's jewellery box. Then she put that with the pictures.

Now she had to go to the police station.

3   ASTRID'S POLICE VISIT

The closest police station was a fifteen-minute walk from Courtney's house in Camden Town. Astrid knew the route well, but she hadn't taken it since she was fourteen. It meant going by the old family home, but she knew it had to be done; this was her city now, and she wouldn't let the shadows of her past impact on what she felt about London.

Every large city she'd visited had loved her like no human ever could. Stepping into rain-strewn streets or striding down cobbled roads was a comfort blanket to her, for they always led to hidden places down dark alleys or deep underground and away from the toil and trouble above. It started for her as a young child, discovering those spots that protected Astrid from the violence at home. They were far from her family and kept her safe even though she was surrounded by those lost to so-called civilised society: the homeless and the drug-addled; the criminals and the drop-outs. But being around them was better than sharing a house with a father who beat her, an alcoholic mother who didn't care, and an older sister who only encouraged their father in his sadism against his younger daughter.

And that's why she'd fallen in love with all cities, for the protection they gave her in their darkest corners. The city welcomed her strident footsteps and cheered her when she culled its more problematic citizens. It reflected her determination in the windows of its skyscrapers; it heard her when she shivered in the winter as the coffee warmed her hands and when she sighed in the summer as the aroma of fresh flowers invaded her senses.

London was in her bones, pulsing through her veins and living in her flesh. Astrid loved the rush of people; the buses and cars honking at each other; the aroma of fried food as she walked past street stands. Even the dirt and pollution were like familiar friends to her.

It was a big, noisy, busy, grimy metropolis, but just around the corner was always a bit of peace. Between the city's skyscrapers were fourteenth-century churches, buildings that survived the great fire of 1666 and Roman walls from two thousand years ago. All life was there. And death and pain and laughter and happiness.

And the missing. Where are the missing? Where are my sister and niece?

She strode through Camden Town, watching the young people milling around The World's End pub, then glancing at The Electric Ballroom and remembering the gigs she'd sneaked into when she was underage. Garbage and Suede were a few weeks apart when she was fourteen in a sweltering summer. After that, as she got older, she hunted out smaller places where she could blend into the background while listening to groups nobody but a handful knew about.

Astrid crossed over the river, watching a narrowboat heading through the lock, remembering the times when she'd spend cold nights trying to sleep on empty barges, or when the dark evenings transformed into mornings, and she was slumbering upstairs on the back of a London bus.

They were memories she rarely returned to, but Olivia and Courtney's sudden disappearance had set her mind going in many directions she didn't want to think about. So she pushed them into the shadows, focusing again on gigs she'd been to, humming along to her favourite Suede song to drown out the echoing sounds of her sister's voice.

It didn't take long to reach the police station, the sight of it resurrecting even more memories from her troubled past. She put them on hold and marched up the steps. Astrid stepped inside and stood at the reception, seeing how the station had changed since she was there as a fourteen-year-old. The layout was different, with plenty of open spaces and shared desks, and the blue paint on the wall smelt and looked brand new. As she waited, she glanced to the far end and the door leading to the interview room where she'd informed his colleagues what type of father Lawrence Snow was.

The queue in front of her included a distressed man dressed as Santa Claus – Christmas was months away – and a middle-aged woman carrying a puppy. The uniformed officer behind the desk looked like an extra from a police TV show, with one of those faces you'd swear you'd seen before. It took him ten minutes to deal with Father Christmas reporting the theft of his sleigh and another fifteen placating the lady with the dog who was upset with her neighbour for a reason Astrid didn't get to overhear. When her turn came, he gave her a forced smile.

'I want to report two people missing.'

His grin disappeared in an instant. She was expecting him to tell her she had to wait twenty-four hours to report a missing person, but she knew that was a myth perpetuated by TV shows and movies.

When she finished giving the few details she had of her sister and niece, Astrid rose to leave. She didn't expect much from the police, but it had to be done. As she considered her next move, a tall uniformed woman approached her. It took Astrid five seconds to recognise her, even though she was older and wearing a different uniform to the one she'd worn during their last meeting in this building two decades before.

'I'm guessing you're not a constable anymore, Jude.'

Jude Thorn pointed to the top of her arm. 'I wouldn't have believed it when I joined the force twenty years ago, but here I am as a Chief Inspector. I thought nothing could surprise me until I saw you here. Is everything okay?'

Astrid ran through her missing persons report again. 'I'd appreciate it if you could give it some priority, Jude. It's not like my sister to just up sticks and leave. I rang Olivia's school, and they said she hadn't attended all week.'

She knew all eyes in the station were on her now. Thorn must have sensed it as well.

'Come to my office and we'll talk about it.'

The longer she was there, the more uncomfortable Astrid felt, but she wouldn't refuse Thorn's offer of help. So she followed the Chief Inspector.

'Would you like a drink?' Astrid raised her eyebrows at the Chief Inspector. 'Nothing alcoholic, I'm afraid. Those days of coppers drinking on duty are long gone, relegated to TV shows and pulp fiction. But I can get the officer to bring us tea and biscuits.'

It was the last thing she wanted. Astrid shook her head and took the seat opposite, considering whether to tell her about the bloodstain in Courtney's bedroom. But that would mean admitting she'd been in the house before going to the station.

'We need to trace Olivia's father.'

Thorn was about to reply when an officer entered and gave her a piece of A4 paper. Astrid assumed it was a copy of the report.

Thorn read the details. 'You haven't seen your sister or your niece in six months?'

'I was in America.'

'Holiday?'

'Something like that.'

'When did you get back?'

'Last week.'

'And you waited until today to see them? Were there any phone calls, texts or emails in between?'

Astrid shook her head. 'No.'

Thorn scanned the report again. 'Your sister wasn't married to Olivia's father?'

'Not that I'm aware of.'

'And you don't know his name?'

'No.'

'You weren't invited to the wedding?'

'It might have got lost in the post.'

'But you and Courtney were reconciled?'

Astrid thought it best not to lie. 'Hardly. You know what she did, how she encouraged him to do what he did.'

Him. Lawrence. Her father and once the superior officer in this police station.

'Is he in touch with Courtney?'

It was a good question, one she'd tried to avoid during her visit to America.

'A few months ago, she told me he was, said he'd spent time with her and Olivia, but I saw no evidence of it.'

'Just like you've never seen or met Olivia's father?'

Astrid twisted in the chair. 'You think my sister might have made all of it up?'

'Well, it's possible Olivia's father has never been involved in her life, and it was all a smokescreen.'

Courtney was an expert liar, but this?

'Why would she do it?'

Thorn glanced at the paper again. 'Perhaps, for whatever reason, your sister didn't want the father involved. She never mentioned him at all to you?'

Astrid shrugged. 'I've spoken to her less than half a dozen times since I left home, and most of those occasions were short conversations.'

Thorn pushed the report away. 'Well, my officers have got enough to make a start. They'll speak to the neighbours, Courtney's workplace and Olivia's school.' She stood and came around the other side of the desk. 'It's strange, you turning up here today, considering what's happening downstairs.'

'Downstairs?'

'Come. I'll give you a tour.'

Astrid followed the Chief Inspector again, feeling like a small dog sniffing at its master's heel. They went down three flights of stairs and into a large room containing a dozen laptops on desks, with operators typing on them. Cardboard boxes, piles of papers and photos surrounded them. They were inputting data, and Astrid had a good guess what it was.

'You're digitising all your old case files?'

Thorn nodded. 'We couldn't have done it without a considerable government grant.' She held out her hands and swivelled her hips to take in everything in the room. 'This is only the reports from the last twenty years, but we'll get to all of it eventually.'

Astrid stood behind a young woman who was inputting data. 'Are my statements in here?'

'Yes, yours and all the others from the investigation into your father. The staff transferred it over only yesterday, which is why I said it was odd you turning up here today.'

She glanced around the room, hearing those fingers hitting all those keys, and considered which of these people knew about the beatings Lawrence had given her.

'Coincidences happen all the time, Jude.' Astrid stared at her. 'Why did you bring me here?'

The Chief Inspector put her hand on Astrid's arm and guided her into the corner.

'No reason, really, but I wondered if perhaps Courtney took Olivia to see your father.'

The same thought had crossed her mind, but she'd preferred not to consider it.

Is that why there's blood in the bedroom?

'Do you know where Lawrence is, Jude?'

She shook her head. 'I haven't seen him since his sentence.'

Astrid snorted laughter so loud, half the people in the room stopped typing for ten seconds before resuming.

'Yes, his three-year sentence, which meant he only did twelve months. Some justice that was.'

'I looked for you afterwards, went to your house and spoke to Courtney. I don't think she was happy with me or the rest of the police. She said you'd run away.'

'I bet she was distraught.' Astrid rubbed at the stitch in her chest. 'Did the police look for me, or was it only you, Jude?'

'I reported it to social services. There wasn't much else I

could do.' She glanced away from Astrid's piercing gaze. 'Do you think Lawrence searched for you on his release?'

'I'm sure he did, but I was well hidden by then.'

Thorn didn't ask where she'd gone after leaving the family home.

'Did you go looking for him?'

'For Lawrence? I didn't need to search for him.' Astrid lifted her shirt, so Thorn saw her flat stomach and perfect abs. 'I don't need to look for him, Jude, because he's always in here. The physical bruises may be long gone, but they still ache here.' She touched her heart and let go of her shirt. 'And in here.' She raised her fingers to her head, staring beyond Thorn towards the rows of computers. 'Do you think there's something in those old papers which might help me find Olivia and Courtney?'

'Do you?'

Astrid pushed past her and put her hand on the door handle.

'No. No, I don't, Jude. Will you ring me if you discover anything?'

Thorn removed a phone from her pocket. 'Of course. Give me your number.'

Astrid did and let the Chief Inspector escort her out of the station.

She watched Jude go back to her job, questioning if her past was affecting her present again.

4 ASTRID'S SEARCH

Astrid found the closest pub, bought two bottles of Mexican lager and retreated to the darkest corner. The bar resounded with hundreds of conversations told in loud voices, all competing with the rock music dominating the atmosphere. Mostly, the crowd was young, students and hipsters, their eyes avoiding her because – she assumed – she was an old woman to them.

But she was glad to be invisible.

She used her phone to check Courtney's social media accounts. The most recent posts were more than a week ago. Her sister had joined the main sites not long after Olivia's birth, so Astrid settled in for a trawl through Facebook, Twitter and Instagram. She ordered two more bottles and some pub grub of steak and chips, of which the meat tasted older than Courtney's internet history, and the chips were paler than a sheep in a snowstorm. The image of a blizzard resurrected memories of the nickname the kids at school had given her. During the difficult times at home, the bigger teenagers picked up on her apparent vulnerability, identifying her as someone they could exploit and torment. But it didn't last for long – her determination to defend herself turned her into a whirlwind of violence the others named Snowstorm. No one had called her that in years, and the childish part of her missed it.

She pushed the thought from her head and concentrated on the task. Twitter was the easiest to go through as Courtney had posted little there. It was all text, with no photos or links to anything else, just her sister's inane political mutterings. She appeared to have acquired their mother's mind set since they were teenagers, parrot-fashioning the ramblings of the *Daily Mail*. Astrid wasn't shocked by Courtney's descent into faux patriotism, but it didn't make pleasant reading.

Did she force these views on Olivia as well?

As she tried to digest her sister's unpalatable opinions, a server brought over her dessert: apple pie with ice cream. She bit through the pastry as she studied Courtney's Facebook page. Most of it wasn't new to her as she'd frequently visited it to check if there were any photos of Olivia. Her sister hadn't used Facebook to put the world to rights, settling on terrible attempts at humour, memes, and occasional comments about work. By the time Astrid had gone through seven years of posts, she'd finished the second set of drinks and the food. She ordered a double gin and tonic before reading Courtney's Instagram posts.

Processing her sister's social media presence attracted a bit of local attention, and Astrid had to fend off approaches from two blokes and one woman. She was cute, but they weren't. It was only a slight distraction as she returned to Courtney's digital life. It was the first time Astrid had looked at her sister's Instagram, relaxing into the pub seat and browsing through posts recording Olivia's life from birth until two weeks ago.

She started with the latest photos, one of Olivia smiling straight into the camera that created phantom fingers clutching Astrid's heart. Then there was an image of her niece riding the bike Astrid had seen at the rear of the house. She ordered another drink as she settled in for a long session.

Astrid was due for a toilet visit when she found something helpful: a post from five years ago; arms holding baby Olivia. Unfortunately, it was impossible to see the adult's face, but Courtney had added text to the image.

Olly's second birthday and a rare visit from Sam

Sam. Astrid saved the photo to her phone and reread her sister's comment.

A rare visit from Sam.

It was only five words, but she had enough experience of Courtney's sarcasm to recognise it in that small amount of text. Was she upset at not seeing him regularly because she loved him, or was it connected to raising Olivia on her own? Perhaps it was a bit of both. Did he work away? Was that why he was rarely with them?

And this was five years ago. Had the situation changed since? Why hadn't she posted more photos or comments about him? Was she with him now, and that's why she and Olivia weren't at home?

Astrid finished her drink as a woman strode into the pub with a dog and carrying a baby. She trawled through the worst parts of her mind for a terrible joke as she realised what she had to do next.

His full name will be on Olivia's birth certificate.

She opened a web browser and located one of the more popular ancestry websites. She created an account and logged in for a free trial. It didn't take long to put Olivia's information into the site, with the results coming back immediately.

She stared at the details, surprised to see the space for the father's name left blank.

Disappointment gripped her throat, so she took a drink to wash it away, but it didn't work. She continued to peer at the screen, ignoring the sound of people having a good time around her, but grimacing when somebody put a Guns N' Roses song on the jukebox.

The pain of the music assaulting her ears forced her mind back to the man whose name she wished had never been on her birth certificate. She listened to Axl Rose moaning about needing time on his own and pictured the last time she'd seen Lawrence as he was taken to prison.

Lawrence. What if he isn't my birth father?

She returned to the ancestry website, hoping it was true, and put in her details, surprised with the answer it gave: *your Search returned zero good matches.*

Astrid tried again, getting the same results.

Your Search returned zero good matches.

Why?

Although there may be many good matches for your ancestor in our content, we can't return good matches without more information.

What should you do?

Add details about your ancestor – even an educated guess can increase your chances of getting a high-quality match.

She added more data, including her mother's and sister's information.

The results were the same.

Zero matches.

Astrid drank more, realising why she was a non-person in the ancestry records.

The Agency. They wiped every digital record of me when I joined their ranks.

She'd always looked upon that disappearance as a good thing, to escape from a world that never wanted her and reappear into a new one of secrecy and espionage where nobody knew the real Astrid Snow.

But now, she wasn't so sure.

The drunks increased in the pub, so she left the bar and headed for the nearest Tube station. Thirty minutes later, she was back in her hotel room and peering at Courtney's Facebook page again. This time, she delved beyond the first posts about Olivia's birth to when her sister created the account.

She had the music on her phone playing through the hotel's Bluetooth speakers as a constant companion, a random playlist she hoped would inspire her to better luck. Not that she believed in such a thing. Luck was for those who couldn't control their lives, and Astrid had been in complete charge of hers since leaving her family behind.

Yet here she was, immersed in their world once again.

But she had no choice, was unable to rest until she found her niece.

Prince serenaded her as she scrolled back to Courtney's first Facebook post, informing the world about starting her English degree at university. Peering at the photo accompanying the text – an image of Courtney looking grim outside her student accommodation, Astrid smiled an ironic grin. Her sister had exhibited little academic potential at school, and it had been Astrid who was always top of her classes.

If I hadn't ended up homeless, would I have gone to university?

She'd had the grades to get to college, and after that, who knows? But her academy had been unlike Courtney's – first Ramon's criminal gang, and then working for the Agency. So now, as she scrolled through Courtney's posts and photos of her university life, she couldn't help but think about how different her life might have been if she'd been born to other parents.

She'd promised herself she wouldn't dwell on her sister's life while doing this; finding something useful to discover Olivia's whereabouts was the priority, but she couldn't help herself. She moved past the photos of Courtney at university, ignoring the images of her sister enjoying herself, and searched for any information on Olivia's father. Astrid rarely read any of the comments on the posts, determined not to get inside Courtney's head. She knew it was a mistake to ignore her Agency training – know your enemy as much as possible – but exploring her sister's personality was something she'd given up on a long time ago. Astrid's work with the Agency had provided valuable insight into the criminal mind, but creeping through Courtney's thoughts held no appeal for her.

I don't want to get inside her head – even though I should.

Astrid scanned the posts while listening to James Brown, Nina Simone, Killing Joke and Blue Öyster Cult. By the time she got to the first Velvet Underground album, she was looking at Courtney's first teaching job, still out of luck with evidence of any man in her life, never mind a prospective husband and father. As Lou Reed was bidding goodbye to the clowns, she needed a break from her sister's world.

It was six o'clock, so she took a walk to the shops and bought a bottle of wine. The drizzle turned into a downpour and she let it wash over her. It wasn't cold, running across her skin like a lover's warm caress. An aroma of cut grass lingered in the air as Bowie's *Low* album hugged her ears. She fiddled with the headphones as water dripped down her cheeks. Someone had once told her that in Bob Dylan songs, rain symbolised memory. If that was true, somebody up there was disposing of an ark full of crappy memories onto her now.

By the time she got back to the hotel, her guts were telling her she needed more than booze. She hadn't eaten since the pub grub, but having only one meal a day wasn't unusual. She'd sometimes fast for days to cleanse her mind and body, another relic of her life in the Snow household. Lawrence had viewed starving his younger daughter as a punishment for an unruly child, but Astrid used it to focus her thoughts. She grew conditioned to it, and food became something she had to endure more than enjoy. Unless she'd had a drink, then it turned into a pleasure.

She poured herself a large glass of Sauvignon Blanc and stared at the photos of her niece's birth on Courtney's Facebook page. Astrid had seen them before, but she examined them now with new eyes. Before, she hadn't given any thought to who Olivia's father was, being only interested in her niece. Now she dug into every like and comment on the posts. Scanning through the first six months of Olivia's life took her down several rabbit holes, but none of them had any light at the end of the tunnel. Progressing through her niece's first three years and finding no mention or photos of the father left her considering something she'd thought doubtful until now.

Did Courtney use a sperm donor for the pregnancy?

She stared at the booze and reached for her phone. Then she ordered Indian food and considered how she might have been right all along about Courtney's unlikely coupling with some unlucky bloke. It would explain many things if it were true.

While she waited for the curry to arrive, she drank a glass of wine, and then poured another before switching her focus from Olivia's father to her sister's friends. The alcohol moistened her lips and warmed her throat as she analysed what she'd seen so far on the Facebook account. Courtney didn't have many friends, which was hardly a surprise, but one colleague appeared in more photos and comments than anyone else.

Astrid reached Olivia's fifth birthday party and the photo of the red-haired woman smiling next to her: Vanessa Moore. She kept trawling through the posts, seeing Moore again, often with her arm around Courtney and grinning. By the time the curry arrived and half the bottle of wine lay inside her stomach, she'd found Moore's home address. As she ate sitting cross-legged on the bed, she discovered everything about Moore that was online: English teacher, thirty years old, native Londoner, no living relatives and, according to her Facebook status, single.

The pillows cushioned her back as Astrid pushed her spine into them. Bits of chicken hung from her lips as she pondered the unbelievable.

Could Vanessa Moore be Courtney's partner? Not in business or crime, but in love?

The laughter surprised her, making Astrid's ribs hurt. She wasn't laughing at her sister's choice in romance, but the fact that, if it was true, she'd never considered this.

Still, I've had maybe three face-to-face conversations with her in over a decade, so how could I be aware of this, especially if she's kept it secret from everyone else?

Wouldn't Olivia have said something the few times we've met?

She cradled the glass in her hand and gazed at a photo of Moore and Courtney on the screen. The only way to find out and discover where her sister and niece were would be to ask Moore.

And now she had the address.

Astrid took one more sip of the wine and got off the bed.

She didn't need the police now.

5 JULIA'S PAIN

Julia was pregnant at seventeen – the result of one night getting carried away with the boy she was teaching to play the guitar. When the elders discovered what had happened, the boy was sent to a different compound, while everyone in The Community looked at Julia differently. Especially the women.

She didn't know why at first. It was not that they didn't want more children in The Community – the opposite was true – but because the elders selected which couples could be together, and that was only if they were married under strict Community rules.

And Julia had followed none of that.

Still, she was happy to be an expectant mother, even if it had come as a shock. Even though the adults looked upon her through disapproving eyes, the people of The Community did everything they could to ensure her pregnancy went as smoothly as possible.

But it was a difficult birth.

The older women took her into the makeshift hospital. They joined The Community doctor to deliver the baby.

Pain gripped every part of Julia as the midwives held her down during labour. Drugs were forbidden, so she had nothing to ease her agony. Even now, many years later, that anguish still possessed her. The sweat and tears covering Julia's face weren't enough to stop her from seeing the disdain on the faces of those who were there to help, and those memories would never leave her.

Every inch of her was inflamed, her eyes burning as she watched the women take her child: a daughter, Sophia. At first, she thought she was hallucinating when she saw her for the first time, as the baby was blue. And she must have been hearing things.

'It's not human,' she heard one woman say.

But Sophia was premature and they took her away for resuscitation. A woman only told her this the following day. For years after – when she wasn't Julia anymore – any time she saw a birth depicted on TV or visited a hospital, it brought everything back to her. The traumatic memories felt less like memories and more like she was still in danger, triggering panic attacks or flashbacks. The nightmares would return, soaking her and the bed with sweat when she woke at three in the morning, her brain searching for a sound in the dark.

More agony was to follow Sophia's birth.

The Community separated children and their biological parents early, and Julia was no exception. She never spoke to the father again, never saw her daughter for the first six months of the baby's life. Only the memories of the pain helped her remember she had a child. She knew better than to ask to see Sophia – that wasn't how parenting worked in The Community.

So she spent most of her time with the other children. There was a building for the kids and a house for adults called the HQ. One night, Julia was eating dinner in the kids' house with two dozen others, with only a few women there to keep them in line, when an adult told her she had to go to the HQ.

The other children fell silent. Being called to the HQ usually meant you were in trouble, and you could get into trouble for any trivial thing, including wearing the wrong clothes, singing "evil" songs, getting caught reading banned books – even walking too close in the street to the opposite sex.

Julia stepped outside, the wind brushing against her face with a cold, harsh touch. They were on different farmland to where she'd found Martin's body, at the other end of the country where Charles Wood had led them after the unfortunate incident – his words – with the police.

Her heart was crawling over her ribs when she stepped inside the big house, the HQ. Hushed tones and suspicious eyes greeted her until The Community's second in command, Paul, approached her.

'Charles needs to see you upstairs,' he said.

Julia clasped at her chest, knowing what this meant. It was a great honour to share a bed with Charles Wood, that's what they were all told, but she didn't think it would happen to her. Not after giving birth to another man's child.

And she was eighteen by then and knew it was no honour.

But it was her Community and she couldn't leave it.

The others spoke about her in whispers as she went upstairs, following the sound of Wood's voice as he repeated the mantra every member of The Community knew off by heart.

We are the One.

And everything flows through Him

To make us all the One.

She stood on the landing, hearing his words but drowning them out with some of her own.

I pushed on Hell's door, fought my way in.
And the Devil feared me
Because I was Woman.

The words echoed through Julia's mind as she saw Wood sitting on the bed when she stepped into the room.

And in his arms was a baby girl.

Sophia.

He smiled at Julia through glittering white teeth.

'Say hello to your daughter, Julia.'

She froze in the doorway, her lips trembling as the song in her head melted deep into her brain. Then strength entered her legs and she inched forward, reaching for the child she hadn't touched for six months.

Wood got up and held the girl out to her.

Julia let the tears slip across her face, feeling the warmth of them transferring to her heart and sparking joy through her whole body.

'Sophia,' she said as she took her daughter in her hands.

She gazed deep into her blue eyes, scared to bring the baby too close to her in case she smothered Sophia in too much love.

But you could never have too much love.

Julia rested her head on Sophia's, letting the tears flow as her smile grew wide enough to sweep them away.

Wood moved forward, putting a hand on Julia's shoulder. She could smell his aftershave, a deep overpowering musk, feel his fingers moving across her skin. But she didn't let that, or him, interfere with her joy of being reunited with her daughter.

'I thought you should have one last moment with Sophia before she leaves.'

The strength seeped out of her legs. Julia struggled to stay on her feet, pushing past him to sit on the bed, still clutching her child.

'She's leaving here?'

He sat next to her. 'You knew this would happen, Julia. The Community always sends the children away to enhance their life experience.'

Every part of her shook. 'Wouldn't she be better off with me, with her mother?'

His smile made the hairs stand up on the back of her neck.

'We're all mothers and fathers here.'

Her tears were not ones of joy, but despair and desperation.

'Where... where will she go?'

Wood shrugged. 'Oh, I don't know yet. I haven't decided.' He stood and loomed over her. 'The Community is growing all the time, Julia. We're not just in England now; we have compounds in Scotland and on the islands beyond.'

She struggled for breath, the weight on her chest threatening to submerge her into the sheets and through the bed. He continued to grin as he held his hands out for the baby. She hesitated until she saw the fire in his eyes.

She gave him Sophia.

Wood held the baby as if she was radioactive.

'Let's hope she's not as troublesome as you were as a girl, Julia.'

She knew better than to argue with him. 'Yes, let's hope so.'

'Who knows, perhaps I'll send Sophia to her grand-parents.'

That weight plunged Julia's heart so far down into her chest, she couldn't breathe. She clutched at her throat, grasping for the words.

'Her grandparents?'

His smile cut right through her. 'Of course. You didn't think I'd force them completely out of The Community, did you?'

'But... but... you banished them for what they did to me.'

He shook his head. 'Children need a stern adult hand; otherwise, they'll become unbearable, like those in the outside world. Your parents might have been a touch excessive, but they're fine now.' Wood gazed right into her eyes. 'Yes, now that I think of it, the best place for Sophia would be with her grandparents.' He moved towards the door before eyeing her. 'I'll give them your best.'

Julia watched him leave before burying her head in the pillow.

That was when she knew she'd make them all pay.

6 ASTRID'S JOURNEY

When Astrid was ten years old, Courtney took her sister's favourite doll and cut it in half using a kitchen knife. Astrid viewed it as a sign to give up childish things and destroyed or gave away all her other toys; all except one – the green-haired Troll she buried in the back garden while imagining that's what she'd do to Courtney one day.

The Snows had long since left the family home - it was sold and converted into student flats ten years ago - but the garden was still there, and she visited it on the way to see Vanessa Moore.

Smoke drifted from the pub next door, and she assumed it was because of an over-excited chef in the kitchen and not because the place was on fire. The burning aroma settled over her like a harbinger of upcoming doom. A train rumbled by on the other side of the fence she'd climbed over, the sound of it on the tracks taking Astrid back to her youth and the times she'd used the noise to drown out her father's anger as his fists rained down on her. There were times she'd hear the train passing by and wish she was underneath it.

But then she grew strong and knew she'd be on the train and far from the Snow family home sooner rather than later.

Now, she rubbed at long-forgotten bruises on her arm as her feet thumped into the grass. The shape of the garden remained the same, a bent circle looking as if a helicopter had landed on it. The only thing different was the rows of fresh flowers planted around the outsides. She inhaled a bouquet of gardenias as she strode to the spot where she'd buried the Troll over two decades ago.

She knelt and placed her hand on the grass, which was damp against her skin. From the age of ten until she ran away at fourteen, she would follow this routine at least once a week, whispering a low promise to repay her sister for all the terrible things she'd done to her. Those promises were stacked high enough to construct a bridge to the moon, but she'd never used them. But she could now if she walked away from Courtney's disappearance and forgot about the blood-stain on the bedroom carpet. And forgot about her niece.

But she could never do that.

She felt the Troll's heartbeat underground and heard its quiet voice whisper to her in her imagination.

Find Olivia.

Astrid climbed over the fence, off to find Vanessa Moore. She looked at the photos she'd saved on her phone from Courtney's Facebook page as she went, peering into Moore's brown eyes and admiring the perfection of her cheekbones. A market was ahead of her, wafting out aromas of exotic spices, unusual perfumes, plus grilled meat and vegetables. It was a cacophony of varied scents, which made her head buzz.

She checked the GPS coordinates for Moore's address, ignoring the chatter from the market traders and listening to her internal soundtrack, a playlist stretching from Nina Simone to Liz Lawrence via a side trip through *Hunky Dory* and *The Hounds of Love.*

By the time Astrid reached the flats, her stomach ached and she was desperate for a drink. She ignored both sensations and walked up the steps, searching for the bell to Moore's flat. A colossal tree leaned over the wall, nearly reaching the road, as if a storm had visited and threatened to uproot it.

She found the address and pressed the buzzer. There was no reply, so she tried it again, getting the same result. She was about to press one of the other buttons when the door opened and a teenage girl came out. Astrid moved inside before the door closed. The place smelt of damp as she went up the stairs to the third floor, stepping over the rubbish and heading for Moore's flat at the end of the corridor.

Astrid knocked three times, getting the same response as with the buzzer. She didn't try a fourth, removing a paper clip from her pocket and bending it at a forty-five-degree angle. Then she got a second clip and twisted it straight before folding it into two, so there was a loop at the end. She took that and pushed it half a centimetre into the lock, twisting the clip to create tension between it and the lock. She held it there and used the clip she'd bent, placing it into the lock and above the other clip and pushing the pins in the lock up. After thirty seconds, it clicked open, and she returned both paper clips to her trousers.

Then she opened the door.

She walked into the living room: brightly coloured three-piece sofa, faded wooden floor, small TV, shelves with plants on them, half-full bookcase, with bright red curtains and art deco prints on the wall.

'Hello, is anybody here?' she said.

Astrid expected no reply and didn't get one. So she looked into the other rooms – a bathroom and single bedroom – finding them empty. She returned to the living room and searched it, checking the books – a mixture of volumes on teaching and a stack of romance paperbacks with gaudy covers – before searching under the furniture and down the sides of the sofa. Again, she discovered nothing useful, so went to the bedroom, looking under the bed before opening the chest of drawers, and then the wardrobe.

At the bottom was a box of photographs. She pulled it out and sat on the bed, removing a handful of images and flicking through them. Each one was of a different woman or girl – sometimes with children – peering into the camera as if they were staring at the devil. She put the first bunch down and went through another group, finding the same: females of all ages and ethnicities with faces worn down by something unknowable. There were no happy smiling people in the photos; no shots of individuals enjoying themselves or relaxing; just countless images of sadness and desperation written large over every face.

The collection of despair transferred itself straight into her, with a sudden weariness possessing her. She returned the photographs to the box, was about to get up and leave when she saw something that made her heart leap. She reached into the bottom of the pile and removed the photo of Courtney and Olivia.

Astrid took a deep breath and scrutinised the image: her sister and niece were grim-faced, sitting in some unknown room, and it seemed to be a recent picture going by how old

Olivia appeared in it. She brought it closer to her, examining every inch, trying to find something insightful in their eyes or the lines on their faces, yet finding nothing.

Then she examined it again. There was a hand at the side of the picture in shadow: a man's hand. Astrid was sure of it. She looked once more, pulling it as close to her face as she could while keeping it in focus. It was a hand, but now she couldn't be sure if it was male or female.

Was it important? Was it Olivia's father's hand, the mysterious Sam?

She scrutinised it again, counting the wrinkles on the skin.

Was it an old man's hand?

Was it his hand?

Was it Lawrence?

Astrid's heart thumped against her ribs and she dropped the photo to the floor.

She left it there for thirty seconds before bending to pick it up, staring at the carpet and remembering the bloodstain she'd seen in Courtney's house.

Astrid put the picture into her jacket and picked up the box. She returned it to the bottom of the wardrobe, wondering why Vanessa Moore had such a collection.

And why did every person in those images look so unhappy?

Including Courtney and Olivia.

She went to the living room, taking a last glance around before leaving and making sure she locked the door behind her. She was heading towards the stairs when someone moved out of the shadows.

'Are you looking for Vanessa? Are you one of her girls?'

The woman was old, with more lines on her face than Astrid saw on the cracked walls around them. She shuffled forward using a walking frame, with only a shabby cardigan and trousers held up by a safety pin covering her wrinkled body.

'Do you know Vanessa Moore?' Astrid said.

The woman's teeth rattled as she spoke. 'I'm her neighbour, Jessica. She always goes to the shops for me, but I haven't seen her in days. Has she gone off with one of her girls again?'

Astrid went to her. 'Why don't you take me into your flat, Jessica, and tell me all about it?'

Jessica's milky eyes narrowed. 'I shouldn't let strangers into the flat, should I?'

Astrid put her hand on Jessica's arm. 'But I'm not a stranger, Jessica. I'm Astrid, Vanessa's friend. Don't you remember seeing me before?'

She peered at Astrid, her top lip trembling as she spoke.

'I don't think I've seen you before, but my memory's not what it used to be.' She scrunched up her face as she gazed at Astrid. 'All those other women and girls Vanessa brought here always looked like frightened rabbits, and you don't look like that; no, not at all.'

Astrid smiled at her. 'What do I look like?'

Jessica returned the grin. 'You look like a wolf about to eat me.'

Her laugh hurt Astrid's empty stomach. 'Well, I am hungry. Do you have any biscuits?'

The smile faded from the woman's face. 'I don't remember.'

Astrid guided her down the corridor and into the flat opposite Vanessa's. It was the same shape and layout, with different furniture and a collection of old photos and frames on the walls. She led Jessica into the chair near the TV.

'Do you live on your own, Jessica?'

Astrid glanced around the room, which appeared clean and smelt okay.

'For a long time now, since my husband died.'

Astrid examined the frames, thinking about the box of photos she'd found in Vanessa's flat. These were different: no colour, all in black and white; a mixture of people and places, and some smiling subjects.

She went into the kitchen, filled the kettle, then looked in the fridge and freezer to find them empty.

'When was the last time you had something to eat, Jessica?'

Astrid sat opposite her while the water boiled.

Jessica rubbed her wrinkled fingers together. 'I had breakfast this morning. My carer did it for me. Such lovely people they are. I don't know what I'd do without them.'

Astrid relaxed into the chair, glad to hear somebody was looking after the old woman. It meant she could concentrate on Jessica's neighbour.

'Tell me about these women and girls Vanessa brought to her flat.'

A glint of life appeared in those tired eyes.

'They were poor women with pain in their faces, at least one every week. I don't know how long they'd stay with Vanessa, but they didn't seem any happier when they left.'

'Did you ever talk to any of them?'

Jessica glanced over at the photos on the wall. 'Oh no, they abandoned me a long time ago. Nobody speaks to me now.' She inched her tiny frame forward. 'Are you my daughter?'

The kettle boiled as Astrid struggled with a reply.

Then she heard the front door open and somebody entered the flat.

'Are you there, Jessie?'

Astrid moved, expecting to see Vanessa Moore, disappointed when a woman wearing a blue uniform came in and plonked two bags of shopping on the floor.

Astrid thought on her feet. 'I found Jessica in the corridor, wandering around dazed and confused. So I brought her in and put the kettle on.'

'Oh,' the carer said. 'Thanks for that.' She went to Jessica. 'We can't have you doing that, Jessie. Do you remember what happened last time?'

'I fell over,' Jessica said.

The carer smiled at Astrid. 'Yes, and you broke your ribs, didn't you? So you had to spend ten days in the hospital, right before Christmas.'

Astrid glanced at the kitchen. 'I'll leave you to it, but the kettle has boiled.'

'Thanks again,' the carer said.

'Before I go,' Astrid said, 'I was trying to get in touch with Jessica's neighbour, Vanessa Moore, but she's not at home or answering her phone. Have you seen her?'

The woman shook her head. 'Sorry, no. I'm not here every day because Jessie has different carers.'

'Okay,' Astrid said. 'One last thing – have you ever seen Vanessa bringing women or girls into her flat?'

Confusion crept over the carer's face to match the look on Jessica's.

'No, I haven't. Why would she do that?'

'I'm not sure,' Astrid said. She smiled at Jessica before she went. 'It was nice to meet you, Jessie.'

The old woman was gazing into her photos on the wall as Astrid left, and she thought again about that box she'd found in Moore's flat.

What has she been up to, and how is Courtney involved?

7 ASTRID'S INTERVIEW

The police were waiting for Astrid outside her hotel. They were plainclothes officers, but she spotted them and their car from fifty yards away. They were out of the vehicle before she reached the steps.

'Astrid Snow?'

'That's me.'

'We need you to accompany us to the station for a voluntary interview.'

'Is this about my niece and sister?'

The tall one with the scar under his right eye shrugged. His gruff exterior matched the look on his face.

'You'll find out more when we do.'

She got into the back of the car without protest. The police officers said nothing else on the journey, and neither did she. On arrival, they marched her into the station and straight to an interview room, where they left her for ten minutes. Astrid wondered if this was Jude Thorn's doing or whether the investigation into Courtney and Olivia's disappearance had already slipped out of her mind.

Then the officers returned and introduced themselves.

The man with the scar was Detective Inspector Coward. It seemed an unfortunate name. His partner was Detective Sergeant Smith. His angular face and narrow eyes reminded her of Iggy Pop in his younger days.

DI Coward placed a file of papers on the table between them.

'We visited your sister's house today, Ms Snow. Can you tell us about the last time you saw her and her daughter?'

Astrid didn't need to think too hard about it. 'Until last week, I was in America for six months. I visited Courtney and Olivia the day before I left the country.'

Coward peered at something in the file.

'And you returned to London with a young American woman, Eve Church.'

'Evie, yes.' A chill gripped Astrid's chest. 'Is this about Evie? Is she okay?'

DS Smith smiled at her. He smelt like an ashtray and she had to hold her breath.

'We're only trying to establish your whereabouts before your sister and niece vanished.'

She pulled her head from him. 'You think I had something to do with it?'

Is this Jude's doing? If so, why?

DI Coward flicked through his papers. 'We have to cover every possibility. I'm sure you understand this, what with your family's connection to the police force.'

Astrid bit hard into her lower lip. 'Are you hinting that Olivia's grandfather is connected to her disappearance?'

The two officers glanced at each other before Coward replied.

'Ms Snow, we have to examine every avenue in the search for your sister and niece. We checked with Courtney's employer and Olivia's school, and they don't know where they are. Neither of them mentioned any problems or issues they might have seen with Courtney or Olivia in the time leading up to their disappearance. And the neighbours weren't helpful either. So we don't have a lot to go on at the moment. Apart from yourself, your father, Lawrence Snow, is the only other living relative.'

The thought of him created phantom fingers that gripped at Astrid's guts.

'Have you spoken to Olivia's grandfather?'

DI Coward shook his head. 'There's no current address for him. Do you have one?'

Astrid pushed the image of *him* back into the shadows of her mind.

'No. What about Olivia's father, Sam?'

The police officers glanced at each other again. DS Smith wrote the name on a piece of paper.

'We didn't have his name until now. What do you know about him?'

'Nothing,' Astrid said. 'I'm not even sure he is Olivia's father. I only found out about him from Courtney's Facebook page.' She leant across the table, seeing the photos of her mother and him – Lawrence – in the file. 'You have checked my sister's internet trail, right?'

She knew from the look on their faces they hadn't.

'Do you have any other names that might help in the investigation?' DI Coward said.

Astrid was about to tell them about Vanessa Moore, but stopped herself.

I can't trust them with anything.

So she gave them something else.

'Courtney's next-door neighbour. She might have seen something.'

DS Smith pulled a paper from the file, and Astrid saw it was a statement.

'We've spoken to Mrs Castle.' He peered straight into Astrid's eyes. 'She told us about the noises she'd heard, sounds of fighting, and she mentioned another interesting thing.'

Astrid knew what was coming, so she got her retaliation in first.

'She spoke to me as well.'

'Yes,' DI Coward said. 'You never mentioned that when you came to the station and made your original report.'

Astrid smiled at him. 'I didn't want to influence your investigation.'

It was a lame excuse, but she couldn't think of anything better.

Coward continued. 'Mrs Castle said you went to the rear of the house. What did you discover there?'

Astrid peered into his eyes, as brown and as frayed as the jacket he was wearing.

'I found a key to the back door, so went inside.'

Both officers fidgeted in their chairs as if hearing what they'd been waiting for. DS Smith glanced at the file of papers.

'Again, you didn't mention this in the initial report you gave to us, did you?'

She let out a long sigh. 'Are you trying to imply something?'

DI Coward smiled at her. 'Can I call you Astrid?'

Astrid nodded. 'Sure.'

He continued to grin through chapped lips.

'Well, Astrid, I'm sure you appreciate that if you don't tell us everything you know, it will make it harder for us to discover what happened to Courtney and Olivia. Wouldn't you agree?'

Astrid ignored his question.

'After the neighbour told me about the sounds of fighting in the house, I thought my sister had been attacked. That's why I checked the back, and when I found the key, I assumed it best to go inside to check if anyone was hurt. But the place was empty. So I came straight to this station to make the report.'

'Leaving out quite a few important details,' DS Smith said.

She didn't answer, wondering how much of her time this was going to waste.

'What is your relationship like with your sister?' DI Coward said.

Astrid placed her hands on her legs under the table, digging her nails into the palms.

'We aren't close. I only stay in touch because of Olivia.'

Coward's smile had vanished. 'Why aren't you close?'

She curled her bottom lip at him. 'Do you have any siblings, DI Coward?'

He nodded. 'I have a brother and two sisters. So we're very close.'

'I'm happy for you, Detective Inspector, but not all families can be as loving as yours.'

DS Smith reached into the file and removed another piece of paper.

'Does the estrangement with your sister have anything to do with the allegations you made against your father when you were fourteen?'

A weight was pressed against her chest now, and all she wanted to do was get out of there. Going to the police had been a mistake.

What else could I have done?

She should have trusted in her Agency training and started her investigation without involving the coppers.

Astrid wiped her hands on her trousers and placed them on the table.

'What has any of this got to do with the disappearance of my niece and sister?'

DS Smith crossed his arms. 'Did anything happen between you and your sister before you went to the United States?'

She gazed deep into his face, seeing the little hamsters running behind his eyes.

Did the police know about the serial killer who had kidnapped Olivia to get at Astrid?

No; if they did, they wouldn't be messing around with these questions.

But Astrid kept the whole truth from them, anyway.

'I met Olivia for the first time, and Courtney said I could keep in touch with her while I was in America.'

'Did you do that?' Smith said.

Astrid nodded. 'I was busy over there, but I'd text and phone her. Sometimes we'd have video chats.'

'And everything was okay?' DI Coward said. 'You never got the impression there might be something wrong with your sister or Olivia?'

Astrid shook her head. 'It seemed fine until I returned and found they were missing.'

DS Smith changed tack. 'Why were you in the US?'

'Just a holiday,' Astrid said.

It would only confuse them to say she'd gone there to return a kidnapped girl to her mother. And then, Astrid had got dragged into so much small-town American crime, she thought she might never return to the UK.

But I made enemies while I was there. Could any of them be involved in Courtney and Olivia's disappearance to get back at me?

'On this holiday, you met this young woman,' DS Smith said. 'Eve Church, and you brought her to London with you?'

Astrid glared at him. 'I've already told you this.'

DI Coward removed a newspaper clipping from the file, and Astrid saw the headline before he unfurled it in front of her.

'While you were in the US, Ms Church's brother was accused of killing two young sisters in the basement of his house.'

She glanced between them, realising they weren't as lazy as she'd first thought.

They've been busy.

'Those charges were dropped against Adam when the police discovered the real killer of those girls.'

Coward pushed the clipping closer to Astrid, who peered at the startled face of Evie from the afternoon someone had tried to blow up her school with her and more than a hundred others inside during a reunion.

'Where is Ms Church now?'

Astrid removed the phone from her jacket and placed it on the table.

'She's in Teesside visiting some distant relatives. I have her mobile number if you'd like to call her.'

DI Coward shook his head. 'When you broke into your sister's house, did you find anything that might indicate where she is?'

'I didn't break into the place, as you well know. And no, I discovered nothing that could be useful in locating them. If I had, I wouldn't have wasted my time coming here.'

She observed their faces while remembering the paper she'd found in the bedroom drawer that was still in her pocket.

'Is there any chance Courtney might be involved in anything illegal, Ms Snow?' DS Smith said.

Astrid couldn't help but laugh. 'Courtney? No.'

Well, nothing apart from encouraging Lawrence to beat me to a pulp most nights when we were kids.

DI Coward returned all the papers to the file.

'We don't want to worry you, Astrid, but there have been reports of increased incidents of people trafficking near your sister's house.'

A dagger shot through Astrid's chest. 'People trafficking?'

Coward's expression was as grim as his clothes.

'There has been a tenfold increase in the number of people identified as victims of modern slavery and human trafficking in London, and over thirty per cent of all cases nationally are discovered in the capital. We've had recent incidents in the area near your sister's place.'

She couldn't believe what she was hearing. 'Victims are usually trafficked into the country, not people who are already here.'

'Things have changed,' Coward said. 'The trafficking gangs have become brazen, especially regarding women and children. I can't go into the details, but there's The Human Railroad, where gangs work together instead of competing. They can move more victims around the country unde-tected and evade our efforts that way. Most of the public – those who bother to take an interest – aren't aware that many people they see or interact with in shops have been trafficked into those jobs and are modern slaves.'

She pressed her palms on the table. 'You think

Courtney and Olivia might be the victims of one of these gangs?'

'We spoke to some of your sister's colleagues at the school where she works. Several of them mentioned Courtney was involved in helping victims of people traffickers.'

Astrid's mind was spinning with all this information.

Courtney helping others? I find that hard to believe.

'Was she involved with organisations who do that work?' Astrid said.

DI Coward shook his head. 'Nobody at the school could help us with that. So we asked the neighbour, Mrs Castle, but she knew nothing.'

Do they know about Vanessa Moore? Is that why all those women and girls were at her flat?

Astrid tried to relax into her chair, but the tension in her muscles stopped that.

'Let me take a wild guess at this – you think my sister might have been helping trafficked people get away from their captors, and that's why she's disappeared? Either on the run or taken by them?'

'It's one avenue we're exploring. The Chief Inspector said we should make you aware of everything.'

So Jude was behind this.

'Is there anything else I should know?' Astrid said.

The officers glanced at each other.

'Not right now,' DI Coward said.

Astrid got up. 'I'll see myself out.'

As she left the station, one incredible thought possessed her.

Maybe Courtney was helping trafficked women and girls.

And she and Olivia were in trouble because of it.

8 ASTRID'S CONFRONTATION

Astrid went to the nearest pub. She ignored the new-fangled places with terrible names and even worse décor, walking into a place that looked like it had been in the city for a hundred years, with most of its customers just as old. She didn't mind, knowing it would be somewhere she could get some peace while she gathered her thoughts.

She bought a pint of cider and slipped into the darkest corner, hearing the clock ticking on the wall, the second hand chasing the minute hand around the face. She placed a finger to her forehead, pressing the imaginary play button on the non-existent jukebox in her brain. Now there were two sounds inside her: the slow beating of her heart and the dulcet tones of Phoebe Bridgers singing about a copycat killer.

The alcohol chilled the back of her throat as she went over everything Smith and Coward had said. All those questions about Lawrence and what Astrid had done at Courtney's place were just their desperation because they had no leads. If they'd checked the house, why hadn't they discovered the bloodstain in the bedroom?

Perhaps they wanted to keep some things from me.

But the people-trafficking angle had thrown her. If Vanessa Moore had been helping trafficking victims – and what the neighbour mentioned about the other women she'd seen with Moore seemed to confirm that – then Moore had got herself in too deep, drawing Courtney and Olivia into its murky world.

The thought of it worried Astrid more than she cared to admit. And it left her in the same position as the police – with no clues where her sister and niece were.

She stayed in the pub until it turned dark outside and the groan in her stomach couldn't be ignored anymore. She stepped into the chill of the gloom, peering at the glittering lights of the bars and restaurants nearby. She could have gone to any of them, but the thought of Olivia forced her to a restaurant the Snow family had a history with. It also made her think again about a question bothering her.

I'd always assumed Courtney had married Olivia's father, yet had never wondered why she'd kept the Snow surname for her daughter.

Yet, deep down, she'd known why her sister had done that.

Courtney kept the Snow name for him, for Lawrence.

Astrid rubbed at her arm before flexing her hands and entering the restaurant. She inhaled seafood aromas and let the server take her to a table. The place was half-full, with a loud bunch of blokes who all looked like they'd gone there straight from selling shares in worthless companies to people who didn't know any better.

She ordered her meal and a bottle of wine to wash it down, the reminiscences of the Snow family outings over twenty years ago swimming through her head. Astrid finished the first glass without it touching the sides, getting a nervous grin from the young woman who'd brought the wine to her. She was halfway through the second drink when her food arrived, knowing the memories would come flooding back and that she was a glutton for punishment for putting herself through this.

But she also hoped it might resurrect some long-forgotten connection between her and Courtney that would help find her missing sister and niece.

I'd be happy just finding Olivia.

A crooked smile crossed her face; she knew how bad that outcome would be for her niece.

I hate Courtney, but I don't want Olivia orphaned. But why not? My life would have been better as an orphan.

She sighed and focused on the food, cracking open a lobster leg in a room full of ghosts. The drunks at the next table spilt wine on the floor, and a server rushed to clean it away. It was all different staff in the restaurant: not one person remained from when her parents had taken Courtney and her there every Sunday night of their childhood.

'It's the family treat,' her mother would always say through bruised lips. She covered the damage behind vibrant red or purple lipstick – something else Lawrence hated.

Her dead mother's voice echoed inside Astrid's head, her thoughts straying between notions of dysfunctional families and those tricked into coming to this country with the promise of helping their loved ones, only to find themselves in situations too horrendous to contemplate. She sucked lobster between her lips as her mind turned to Vanessa Moore.

I bet nobody has reported her missing.

She was considering revisiting Moore's flat when

someone screamed from the kitchen. It took her a second to realise it was a girl's voice. She dropped the crustacean from her fingers and jerked towards the sound of distress. The boozed-up blokes near her leered and jeered as she pushed by them. Their insults joined the others stacked in her memories as she strode through the kitchen door where a teenage girl lay sprawled on the floor. She wore a cleaner's uniform, the fear in her eyes burning as she glanced to the side. Astrid turned to see a big man snarling as he wielded a shining knife. She guessed he was the head chef.

He pushed his face into hers. 'No customers allowed in here.'

An aroma of garlic and onions swept over her as he sizzled, his cheeks bellowing a fiery red as the blade wobbled in his hand. The heat increased in the room as she grabbed his wrist and snapped it back; it cracked more easily than the lobster leg had. His scream shattered the shadows in her head, scattering childhood images around every corner of her skull. The chef whimpered, but all Astrid saw was her sister encouraging their father's sadism. She let go of the crying man and he collapsed to the floor.

Astrid went to the teenager.

'Are you okay?' The girl nodded as a sudden thought pinged into the front of Astrid's brain. 'Are they forcing you to work here?'

The girl didn't reply, but Astrid observed the answer in her eyes. She jumped from Astrid, barged through the door and into the restaurant. Astrid let her go and returned to the chef writhing on the tiles.

'Where do you get your staff from?' she said to him.

Fear gripped his eyes. 'I'm only the cook. I don't hire anyone here.'

She peered into his face and knew he was telling the truth.

How hard would it be to track trafficking gangs local to Courtney's house? Or Moore's flat?

It was a slim lead, but it was better than nothing.

Astrid returned to the table and threw money down as she checked her phone, staring at a photo she had of Olivia. The drunks yelled insults at her when she left, while she focused on the image of her niece. Drizzle drifted across the air as she stepped outside.

Perhaps if I talk to those two coppers again, Coward and Smith, they might point me towards one of these trafficking gangs.

It was that or return to the restaurant tomorrow to speak to whoever hired its staff. Or talk to the girl who'd run away.

Astrid considered both options as she walked to the hotel, letting the rain settle on her face and bring some freshness back to her brain. She'd had a fair amount of drink, but she knew that wouldn't interfere with the way her mind worked.

As long as I don't get into any fights, I should be okay.

That thought stuck to her head as two slabs of brick shithouse approached, both as bald as each other with faces not designed for conversation. They smelt of cheap aftershave and terrible tattoos, of days spent behind bars and collecting bad debts.

The one with no eyebrows spoke to her.

'Come with us, Snow.'

They stood a few feet from her, but she didn't move. The street was empty apart from a homeless man sleeping in a doorway and a pigeon perched on a wheelless car.

'Some other time, boys. I've got a date with a bottle of wine, and you two don't look like you drink rosé.'

They looked at each other, and then back at her. No Eyebrows was faster than he appeared, flicking a shoulder out so his hand was on her before she could react.

'This isn't a negotiation, lady.'

He squeezed her arm for added emphasis.

'You're right; it isn't.'

Astrid struck her palm into his throat. His Adam's apple trembled as he tumbled into the wall. His twin's reactions were slower than his, which was enough for her to bring her leg around and kick him in the knee. He crumpled like a cheap suit, his agonised cry scaring the pigeon away in a burst of flapping feathers.

No Eyebrows was out for the count with a sparkling new bruise covering his throat. She guessed he wouldn't be saying much of anything for the next few days. Or eating any solid food. The other bloke clutched at his shattered kneecap and groaned as he squirmed on the ground. She stared at them and imagined they were some giant human worm separated by shared pain.

She stood over the one still awake.

'If the medics get to you quickly, they might save your knee. But, even then, you won't be walking for a while.'

He fumbled in his pocket, grasping for a phone he dropped because his fingers shook so much. She knelt and picked it up.

'Call for an ambulance.'

The words crawled over his lips. She ignored his request and went through his contacts, but found nothing illuminating.

'Who sent you?'

Astrid did a quick calculation of how many people in London she'd upset in her life; just London, not the rest of the country – that would have taken far too long. When she settled on a number, she realised it could be one of several who'd directed these lugs to intimidate her, but nobody who knew her would have done something so stupid. Only someone who hadn't met her before would be clueless enough to think these two slabs could frighten her.

She dropped the phone just out of his reach and asked again.

'Who sent you?'

He screwed up his eyes. 'Mr Scorpio wants to see you.'

'Scorpio?' She didn't know anyone by that name, one you wouldn't forget. 'He sounds like a bad Bond villain.'

Even through the agony, he grinned. 'You won't say that when you meet him.'

'And why would I do that?'

He inched back like a crab. Astrid was impressed with his agility, considering how much pain he must have been in.

'You will if you want to see your sister again.'

Electricity stabbed at her chest as she glanced between them, her mind running through the permutations of why these goons would be interested in Courtney. The process helped control the rage growing inside her, her blood transforming into lava, the top of her head now a kettle ready to boil.

Why would a schoolteacher be involved with thugs like this? Where is Courtney? And is Olivia safe?

She glared at him. 'Where were you going to take me?'

He hesitated for only a brief second. 'We have to take you there.'

Astrid laughed at him. 'How far will you get with that busted knee?' She put her foot near his mobile. 'Tell me where this bloke is and I'll let you have your phone.' She used her smile to contain the fire raging inside her. 'We were going there anyway, weren't we?'

His fingers trembled near the phone, but not close enough.

'There's a pub around the corner, The Pit and the Pendulum, but everyone calls it The Pit. He's waiting for you in there.'

Her anger reduced a little as she laughed. 'The Pit and the Pendulum? Did Halloween come early this year?'

Spit dribbled over his lips as he coughed. 'It hasn't always been that. It's been there years, but this isn't my manor, so I don't know what it's like.'

Astrid kicked the phone at him as his colleague opened his eyes and groaned. She left them there, marching down the street and around the corner to look for this gothic pub.

It didn't take long to find it since she'd been inside the place many times before. The last time was on her twenty-first birthday when it was called The Dog and Duck, and she'd snapped a pool cue over a bloke's head.

And it was the last time she'd seen Ramon, the guy she'd been living with for six months right until that birthday night.

Ramon Sheen: the man who'd introduced Astrid to the world of organised crime.

The man who believes I betrayed him.

She stepped into the pub and wondered if the pool table was still in the same place.

9 JULIA'S REVELATION

Losing Sophia brought another change to Julia's life in The Community.

She was still living on the same farm when Paul, the second in command behind leader Chris Wood, announced to the commune she was to be treated as an adult – a child no more. Julia wondered if it meant she'd get different work duties, or something much worse if it were her time to marry one of the elders: a pairing with a man she didn't know who she'd be expected to provide with as many children as possible. The elders had told Julia that Sophia was a "mistake" because they hadn't sanctioned it, so they'd rectify that with an authorised relationship – one she'd have no say in.

But that wasn't to be her fate yet as she was introduced to something even more bizarre – the real reason Wood had founded The Community.

She'd just finished milking the cows when Paul approached her.

'It's time for you to learn the truth about The Community, Julia.'

She gazed at the darkness in his face, watching it contrast with the light flickering in his eyes. Julia dropped the bucket and it cracked against her shin.

'Is it Sophia? Have you brought her back to me?'

He shook his head. 'It's much more important than that.'

The wind cut across her face as more elders came out of the shadows. Paul took her hand and led her into one of the larger buildings in the commune – somewhere off-limits to all the children. She didn't know what to expect – perhaps they were about to give her somebody else's baby to raise. But when she strode inside, it was to the sight of a group of adults sitting cross-legged around a large triangle. It was only as she got closer to it she saw Charles Wood sitting in the middle.

'Welcome, Julia,' he said.

Paul took her into the triangle to sit opposite their leader. The mud stuck to her fingers as she sat, peering into his wide eyes.

'Is this about Sophia?'

Wood smiled at her. 'In a way, yes, because this is about all of us.' He placed his hands on hers. 'We, the elders, have tried to keep you and the other children safe from the outside world until you're old enough to realise how dangerous it is. Do you understand that, Julia?'

His skin was warm against hers, and it sent a shudder down her back.

'Yes.'

'You've visited the village nearby, and you know how humans are destroying this planet.' She nodded. 'Good. The outsiders are trying to rectify their mistakes, but it's too late for that.' He gripped her fingers. 'But you needn't worry about that because The Community contains the chosen ones to be saved.'

'Chosen by who?' Julia said.

Wood let go of her and stood. 'Many years ago, creatures from beyond this world – the Chi – visited me and told me how a small select group of humans were to be saved from ecological disaster and transported from this dying planet. I am their disciple and your leader, here to guide The Community to a better life off this world.'

Julia listened to his words, wondering how she hadn't been aware of this strange notion before. She was told that all the sightings of UFOs and tales of alien abductions were real, part of the preparation. World governments knew what was happening, but kept it from the public to prevent global panic.

'Will I see Sophia again?'

'Yes,' he said. 'As long as you behave and follow the rules.' His grin unnerved her. 'Know your place in this world, Julia, if you're to have one in the next world.'

What could she do but agree with him? She knew it was nonsense, but was prepared to do anything to be reunited with her daughter. So she listened as they discussed the forthcoming apocalypse and how the Chi would help The Community escape it.

The other adults took her outside into the large field behind the building when they'd finished talking. There she saw a larger version of the triangle – it represented the UFO that would spirit them away – and Wood led them all inside. It was made of wood and must have taken a long time to build. Once inside, Julia could smell jasmine and incense as Wood got them to sit on the floor, all holding hands while they sang that familiar song.

We are the One.

And everything flows through Him
To make us all the One.
We are the One.
And everything flows through Him
To make us all the One.

She joined in with them, unsure if "the One" and "Him" were the same and if they were both Charles Wood. The singing lasted all night until the stars glittered above them and, from exhaustion, Julia thought she saw the lights turning into hovering UFOs.

When she could finally leave, she was turning to go to her bunk with the other children until Paul stopped her.

'You're a woman now, Julia.'

She wondered why she wasn't one before, when she'd given birth to Sophia.

But she didn't tell him that.

'Where will I sleep?'

She knew from the look on his face where it would be.

He led her out as she glanced at the other women for help, but their heads were lowered. The buzzing in her brain continued all the way to his house, her eyes avoiding his and fixed on the sky as she wanted the Chi spaceships to come and take her away. She pulled from him when they reached the steps – there was nothing left to lose by being brave now.

'Do you think aliens are coming to save us?'

He narrowed his eyes at her. 'You don't believe climate change is making the planet unliveable for humans?'

'Of course,' she said, 'but that doesn't mean aliens will take us away in spaceships.'

Paul held out his hands. 'The evidence is everywhere, Julia. We don't tell the children because we don't want to scare them. That's why we wait until you're eighteen.

You're an adult now – a woman – so you must understand the reality of this world.'

'If I'm an adult, why can't I make my own choices?'

He shook his head. 'Who's stopping you from doing that?'

She glanced at his house. 'I don't want to go in there.'

His cheeks turned a fiery red. 'You're refusing to come with me, second only to our leader?'

Julia twisted her hands into fists. 'I am.'

He laughed. 'No, you're not.'

Paul grabbed her arm and pulled her towards him. She wriggled out of his grip, but he grasped her again. Julia forced her shoulder into him and shoved. He let go and stumbled over. She watched him fall and guessed what he'd do next. He jumped up and glowered at her, spit dripping from his lips as he reached for her.

She punched him in the face.

Her knuckles throbbed as his nose broke. He staggered back and fell to the ground.

Julia stood over him, her heart beating like a runaway train.

That was the night her life changed again.

The name may have changed, but nothing much else had in over a decade: dark-patterned carpeting, textured walls and an odd mixture of ornaments – knick-knacks you might find at a jumble sale, old framed photographs, and several plaques containing the names of people who'd won various indoor sporting events over the years, especially darts, pool, and dominoes. Astrid wondered if the one with her name engraved on it was still in the pub somewhere. She took a deep breath, smelling the ale and cider in the air. It didn't linger long, replaced with the sickly sweet smell of someone's vape.

After she'd left home, Astrid had lived on the streets until she met Ramon, and he'd taken her under his wing. And this was the place where they'd spent most of their time together. Even when he'd convinced her to use her hacking skills to steal for him, it was in the shadowy corners of this pub where she'd completed those tasks. She also gained her love of cider here and discovered tunes released long before she was born.

She looked across the room, seeing if the jukebox was

still there. It wasn't, but a newer version had replaced it. Astrid went to it, amused to see she could pay for the songs using an app on her phone. Most of the music was more Radio One friendly than her usual tastes, but several classic albums were listed. She selected five tracks before heading to the bar to get a drink.

The visit to the jukebox wasn't only for nostalgia, but to scope out the place, searching for the mysterious Mr Scorpio, even though she didn't know what he looked like. What had once been the bar and the lounge had been knocked through into one large room.

And the pool table had gone the way of the dodo.

She bought a pint of cider and pretended to be searching for somewhere to sit as Lou Reed's gnarly voice broke out of the sound system. There was a group of four grey-haired men in the far corner, putting the world to rights and moaning about the state of their health. Beyond that was a young couple, probably in their twenties, holding hands with the woman looking anguished at the music wafting around the pub.

Astrid thought that was it until she saw someone sitting in the spot where she'd spent her time breaking through the security of financial institutions and government organisations; somebody she recognised.

She took her drink and didn't wait for an invitation to sit opposite him. His wrinkled face beamed at Astrid as his spotted hand rubbed at the delve in his cheek.

'Well, well, fancy my tired eyes seeing a Snowstorm at this time of the year.'

'You know I don't like that name, Bob.'

He shook his withered head at her. 'I thought you might have grown to like it after all this time.'

Whispering Bob Mandela had acquired his title in three

parts. The first was because his voice was so quiet, the only way you could hear him was by leaning into his face, which presented several problems, the worst being you'd get a flash of his yellowed teeth while giving him the room to grab you by the neck and squeeze the life from your throat. His name was Robert, which accounted for the Bob bit, and Mandela was because he'd spent twenty years in prison for his political beliefs. That was where he'd met Ramon Sheen and taken him under his wing. Bob also mentored Astrid when she entered Ramon's orbit and became an essential part of his criminal gang.

'I'm surprised to see you still here, Bob, especially looking like that.'

He grinned at her. 'You mean alive?'

She didn't, and he knew it. When Astrid had first met him in this pub, Bob was suffering from a painful skin condition on his face, like an extreme case of acne. Others around him never mentioned it, but she was direct.

So she'd asked him about it. He told her about the brutality of his two older brothers and his parents' cruel indifference, and these seemed to have been the major themes of his childhood. His mother and father were alcoholics and gamblers, which shadowed his whole adolescence, and affected Bob through his father, who took out his frustrations on his wife and sons. He described his father's terrible beatings to Astrid, inflicted for minor transgressions like missing a blade of grass when he mowed the lawn. When Bob reached puberty and broke out in a world-class case of acne, he saw it as a symptom of his helpless suffering.

'The poisoned life exploded out of me, all my suppressed screams spouting out in another form.'

Astrid knew he'd never mentioned it to anyone before,

and she responded by relating to him what Lawrence had done to her, plus Courtney's encouragement of the abuse and her mother's indifference to it all. It created an instant bond between them she was sure neither had found with anybody else.

'Have you even moved since the last time I was here?' she said.

'You mean when you cracked Ramon's skull with that pool cue?'

She smiled. 'Your voice and your face are back to normal.'

He laughed through those yellow teeth. 'You can't use the word normal anymore, Astrid, not when describing people. It implies they were abnormal before.'

'You know what I mean, Bob. You could hardly speak above a whisper before.'

He ran a long fingernail over his Adam's apple as if he was a vampire inspecting his latest victim.

'My throat had been damaged when I was a kid during one of my father's usual episodes. I only found out decades later after visiting the doctor because I thought I had cancer.'

Astrid sipped at her drink. 'And they fixed it?'

'There was a tiny piece of plastic stuck there – been there for forty years – and they removed it.'

She shook her head. 'It's a day of strange revelations.'

'You got that right,' he said. 'What are you doing here after all this time?'

She didn't mince her words as the Thin White Duke sang about throwing darts into lovers' eyes.

'Are you still involved in organised crime?'

He jerked forward and spat beer over the table.

'I'm sixty-five years old, Astrid. I can barely walk fifty

yards without pain taking over most of my body, and I have to go to the bathroom every twenty minutes. What do you think I could do in a criminal gang?'

She checked the lines under his dark eyes. 'Maybe run one?'

Bob's laugh rattled his teeth. 'Oh, I have missed you, Snowstorm.'

'You're not denying it.'

He finished his whisky, the smell of it drifting from his lips and over to her.

'Families run top-level organised crime, and that's something I don't have anymore.' He glanced across at the young couple on the other side of the pub. 'It's either that or low-level wannabe gangsters dealing in street drugs. What they earn wouldn't have paid for Ramon's weekly spend on clothes back in the day.'

Ramon. Astrid knew she'd have to talk about him, but not yet.

'You still have your nose to the ground, don't you, Bob? So you know what's going on around here.'

He cradled the empty glass in his hand. 'It's not like it used to be. People were violent then, we both know this, but there was a code of honour, so only other criminals got hurt, not ordinary folks and the innocent.' His lips trembled as he spoke. 'Nowadays, it seems like everyone is fair game, with kids stabbed for something as stupid as disrespecting some gangbanger or low-life drug pusher.' He glanced at the other people in the pub. 'I could go to the bar and stumble into some young punk, and he'd stab me in the eye just for that.'

Bob shook his head, and she saw his face filled with nostalgia for the days when he and his friends were on top of the criminal hierarchy.

'I'll get both of us another drink.'

She got up and went for the drinks as *The Last Of The Famous International Playboys* came hurtling out of the jukebox. Bob was picking food from his teeth when she returned and dropping it on the carpet.

He took the double whisky from her. 'Thanks, Snowstorm.' He grinned when she grimaced. 'Is that why you're here, for a catch up on the local glamour you've missed in the last decade?'

'I'm looking for someone called Scorpio.'

She watched his eyes narrow as he lifted the glass to his mouth. Liquid clung to his lips when he took the whisky away.

'That's just a name, a myth the old lags put around to frighten the kids. And by old lags, I mean those in their twenties. Some aren't even into their teens before they're one of the gang.'

'If Scorpio is a myth, then why did two thugs use his name when they came for me?'

He cradled his drink and shrugged. 'They probably wanted to scare you.'

'They wanted to bring me here to see him. And they knew me, but I didn't know them.'

He looked Astrid up and down as if they hadn't been talking for ten minutes.

'Perhaps your past has come back to haunt you.'

'It never left me, Bob.' And she didn't want to talk about it now. 'Who's in charge nowadays?'

He opened a packet of prawn cocktail crisps and offered them to her. She shook her head.

'It's changed a lot since you were last here, that's for sure.' He crunched on a crisp, the aroma of its chemical components generating an overpowering smell of fake prawns. 'An explosion in counterfeit goods and drugs –

particularly cocaine – with the rise in new technologies has eased the flow of money, communications, commodities and people across the city. There are people out there drinking bottles of untaxed Italian wine smuggled in by the Sicilian mafia who've moved into London. There are owners of empty factories who wake up one morning to find their land buried under tonnes of rubbish, victims of an illegal waste-disposal industry worth billions a year.' Bob glanced at the dirt on his fingers. 'I know people who get their nails done in a salon or their car washed by hand at pop-up garages in a car park, oblivious to the fact they're being served by someone who has been trafficked.' He nodded at the young couple as they went to the jukebox. 'Even the system playing that music is dodgy, having been brought over from the Far East, skipping the payment on customs and excise.'

Astrid had the taste of cider on her lips when she spoke.

'Organised crime has diversified; I understand that, but tell me what you know about people trafficking in the city.'

He shook his head. 'I only know what I see in the news: people smuggled into the country from abroad, told they're going to get a decent job, then charged huge amounts of money they have to pay back through modern slavery or by being forced into prostitution.'

'Are you aware of any gangs in the area involved in that?'

'No,' he said. 'Why do you ask?'

She reached over and took one of his prawn crisps.

'And you've never heard of a Mr Scorpio?'

'I told you, Astrid, that's an old name, one that was around even before you met Ramon and his gang. Old-timers would use it like parents who frighten their kids by saying there is a bogeyman. If you don't behave, Scorpio will get you; that sort of thing.'

She slipped the crisp into her mouth, talking as she ate.

'If that's so, how come I've never heard of it before?'

He laughed at her. 'You were far too busy back then, Astrid, either on that laptop of yours all the time or wrapping your lips around Ramon and letting everybody know about it.'

The taste of prawn shocked her throat. 'I was young and naïve then. I soon stopped doing both and moved on to better things.'

He ran his hand over the crisp packet. 'Perhaps this Scorpio thing is someone getting back at you after all this time.'

'Getting back at me for what?'

Bob's bones rattled as he grinned. 'Come on, Astrid. Not only did you dump Ramon and disappear not long after that, but the coppers arrested most of the gang. So many people didn't believe the two things were unconnected. And a lot of them hold grudges.'

She washed the taste of the prawn crisp from her mouth with a swig of cider.

'That had nothing to do with me, Bob. Anyway, I heard Ramon left the country once I'd gone.'

He shrugged. 'You broke his heart. That's why he ran away. No one knows where he went, but there were rumours about Spain or Mexico.'

Astrid listened to Dua Lipa singing about wanting to be alone.

'I never told Ramon or anybody where I was, but somehow, I'd get Christmas cards from him for the first few years.' She peered at Bob. 'Do you know where he is now?'

He shook his head. 'I don't even know if he's alive. Do you think he's your mysterious Mr Scorpio?'

She pushed her back into the seat and finished her drink.

'I doubt it, but it's a bit of a coincidence those two thugs send me to this pub – even with its new name – and then I find you in here.'

Bob held out his hands. 'I'm in here every night of the week, Astrid. I have no family or friends left. This is the only place where I can get any company these days. And it's much warmer than my manky flat.' He pulled a face at the sounds coming out of the jukebox. 'Though some of the music leaves a lot to be desired.'

She got up. 'At least I know where to find you if I need to speak to you again.'

He raised his drink to her as she left the pub. 'Anytime, Snowstorm.'

She stepped outside, no further forward in finding her niece and sister than when she went in.

Only to be greeted by another welcoming committee.

11 ASTRID WALKS A DOG

There were four of them waiting for Astrid in the rain. She recognised the two blokes in their forties who had been Ramon's most trusted lieutenants until she came along. The one at the front was Boris, six foot six of pure muscle and the brain to go with it. He pointed a fist at her.

'We've waited a long time for this, Snow.'

She stared at the man next to him, a foot smaller and twice as nasty – Jacko. He had a knife in his hand. The other two were unknown to her, younger but also carrying blades.

'Do I owe you money, Boris?'

Jacko snarled at her. 'You owe us more than that, bitch.'

Astrid sighed. 'Four of you, three with knives, all for me?'

Jacko waved the blade at her. 'Five years we spent behind bars because you went to the coppers.'

'That wasn't me.' She ignored the knife, staring at Boris. 'How many of the old gang did the police arrest?'

'How many? All but you and Ramon.'

She kept looking at them as she spoke, her mind working out how to deal with these idiots.

'What happened to Ramon?'

Boris glanced at Jacko. 'The rumour was you topped him and buried the body.'

Astrid laughed at his words. 'Why would I kill him?'

He pointed at the pub behind her. 'The last time anybody saw Ramon was when you attacked him with that pool cue. Then, the next day, both you and he vanish just as the coppers nick the rest of us.' He inched towards her. 'The evidence they had to convict us came from somebody's computer, and the only person I ever saw with one of those was you.'

'What happened to all the money?' she said.

He shook his head. 'The coppers took that with them.'

'No,' Astrid said. 'Not the physical cash, but the digital transfers I stole from Cayman Islands banks for Ramon.'

Boris snorted at her. 'I don't know what you're talking about. Only you and Ramon were involved in that hi-tech stuff.'

Her smile reflected off the knife Jacko waved at her.

'So, the day you and the others are arrested, Ramon disappears the same time millions of pounds do as well.'

'Don't try to blame him for what you did, Snow.'

Jacko was close enough now for her to act. She moved forward and grabbed his wrist, twisting it to the side, so he dropped the blade. Jacko squealed as the knife hit the pavement, and she pushed him back into the two younger blokes. Astrid kicked the weapon away as they caught her would-be attacker.

She peered straight into Boris's face.

'You're clever, Boris, so think about it. I didn't know Ramon wasn't telling you about what I stole; he said he'd share it with all of us. Yet, he and the money vanish on the same day somebody provides the police with the evidence to arrest everybody else.'

'At the same time, you pull your vanishing act,' Boris said. 'You whose old man was a high-ranking copper.'

Astrid shook her head. 'My old man was disgraced by then, and I hated the police as much as any of you. I left because I'd had enough of Ramon. I didn't care about the rest of you.' She smiled at him. 'No offence.'

'Why did you hit him with that pool cue?'

She kept one eye on Boris while noticing Jacko glaring at her.

'Ramon was always groping me, even after I'd told him it was over between us. He wouldn't listen, hence the pool cue.'

Jacko stumbled forward. 'You're saying Ramon grassed us all up to the pigs and ran off with that money you stole?'

'If you think about it long enough,' she said, 'even your empty head will see the truth of it.'

'The pigs will know what happened,' Boris said.

She nodded. 'I expect so.'

He narrowed his eyes at her. 'Which means you can get the truth for us, Snow.'

'Why would I do that?'

Boris laughed at her. 'Because then we'll let you live, that's why.'

She didn't agree or argue, stepping past him and the others. Astrid ignored their mutterings and set off down the road. Her original intention had been to go back to the hotel, but this encounter with Boris and his cronies had sparked a new idea in her head. So she turned in the other direction, hoping the Chief Inspector was still living in the same house Astrid had visited when she was fourteen.

FORTY MINUTES LATER, she was ringing the bell at the front door, which hadn't changed in more than a decade. Jude Thorn didn't seem surprised when she opened up to see Astrid standing there.

'Is this about DI Coward's interview with you?'

'That and some more. Can I come in?'

'No,' Thorn said. 'We're going out. I have to take Flossie for a walk.'

'Flossie?' Astrid said.

The answer came running towards her, a small, fluffy white dog looking like a giant cotton wool ball bouncing up and down. Thorn put a lead on the mutt, then dragged it outside and locked the door.

'There's a park around the corner. We can talk there.'

Astrid followed her, thankful the rain had stopped. The streetlights flickered as they went, casting an unusual illumination on the two women. There were still a few people about, so she kept her thoughts to herself until they reached their destination. Thorn removed the lead and let Flossie chase after phantom squirrels when they got to the gate.

'This is very cloak and dagger, Jude.'

Thorn's grin seemed crooked under the moonlight.

'That's ironic, considering your past.'

They ambled along the path and moved deeper into the park.

'What do you mean?' Astrid said.

Jude stopped as her mutt took a dump on the grass.

'You think I don't know about you working for the Agency?'

The shadows appeared to surround Astrid as the dog stank the park out.

'What agency was that?'

Jude grinned at her. 'Please, Astrid, don't take me for an idiot. The only reason you didn't end up in prison with the rest of Ramon Sheen's criminal gang was because you were recruited into the clandestine government organisation most people don't know exists.'

'So, how do you know about them?'

'I'm a Chief Inspector in the police, so I get to know some of the government's dirty little secrets. I admit I didn't know about your recruitment when it happened, but I found out a few years later. It was a surprise to think of you as a paid assassin, but I suppose it was understandable.'

Astrid didn't dissuade Thorn from thinking she was an assassin – even though she wasn't. It allowed her to ask a question she'd prepared for the Chief Inspector.

'Who provided the evidence that convicted Ramon's gang?'

'I can't tell you that, Astrid.'

'It was fourteen years ago, Jude. They've all been released by now.'

Thorn nodded. 'Indeed. I'd assume some of them might look for revenge against whoever grassed on them.'

'It wasn't me.'

'I know that.'

And that confirmed what Astrid had told Boris and his goons.

'So it was Ramon. What happened to him and the stolen millions?'

'I can't confirm or deny who it was that helped convict Mr Sheen's gang, but I will say that the person now has a comfortable life in another part of the world.'

Astrid pushed the thought of Ramon from her head.

'Do you have any updates on Courtney and Olivia?'

'Sadly, no,' Thorn said. 'Though it took you a long time to ask about them.'

She ignored the jab. 'Coward seemed to think I might be involved in their disappearances.'

Thorn shrugged. 'They have to investigate all avenues.'

'Including people trafficking?'

'What do you know about that?'

Astrid told her what she'd discovered at Vanessa Moore's flat.

'Courtney and Moore worked at the same school and were friends. If Moore was helping trafficked women and girls get away from their captors, perhaps Courtney got drawn into that world.'

'Why didn't you tell DI Coward this?'

'He and his mate seemed too preoccupied with confirming my guilt, and I thought I'd get a lead quicker than they would.'

'But you haven't?'

'Have you heard of a gangster called Mr Scorpio?'

'Why do you ask?'

'That means you have, right? What can you tell me about him?'

Thorn started walking again, leaving her dog's shit steaming in the grass.

'Scorpio used to be an old wives' tale, one of those scare stories you told to stop your kids getting into trouble.'

'Used to be?' Astrid said.

Flossie scampered around their legs while her mistress spoke.

'A few years ago, the name popped up in statements from women we'd rescued from trafficking gangs. At first, we thought it was just another extension of the scare stories – you might think we're bad, but if you don't behave, Mr Scorpio will visit you, and you won't like that – that type of thing. But then the NCA – the National Crime Agency – that deals with people-trafficking gangs got more information, which appeared to indicate Scorpio was a real person.'

'Do you have a name for Scorpio?'

Thorn shook her head. 'No, but I can tell you who is the biggest trafficker in the city.'

Astrid watched the dog sniffing at a post. 'Go on.'

'He's a property developer and millionaire business-man, Paul Jagger, who runs a large organisation selling drugs and people.'

'So why haven't you arrested him?'

'That's simple: we have no evidence.'

'How do you know he's a criminal?'

'Because we had people come forward from inside his crime empire, and they told us enough to convince the police of his guilt.'

'What happened to these informers?'

'Both of them disappeared before they could provide the evidence we needed. And they weren't the only ones to vanish.'

Astrid recognised the pain in her eyes.

'You had an officer undercover in his organisation.'

She nodded. 'Detective Constable June Ritchie. Jagger's name isn't on anything illegal – most of his businesses are shell companies used to avoid paying tax. The main busi-ness is Jagger Properties, and then under that is a great spider's web spinning off into a dozen different directions. We can tie him to retail shops, food distribution, manufac-turing and clothing. But none of the stuff he uses to launder money.'

'So where does DC Ritchie fit in this?'

'She got a job as an accountant in one of his factories to gain the trust of the underlings who run Jagger's empire.'

'And she disappeared?'

Thorn nodded. 'Three months ago.'

'Just like my sister and niece.'

'People disappear all the time, Astrid, especially in London. It doesn't mean the two cases are connected.'

'Vanessa Moore has vanished as well.'

'Do you know this teacher?'

'No. I found the connection through Courtney's Facebook. Then a neighbour told me Moore hadn't been seen in a week.'

'Just like your sister and niece.'

'Indeed. Too much of a coincidence, don't you think?'

'And you believe Scorpio is involved?'

'I've no idea. I'm only going on what those thugs said to me. I got no information on this Scorpio from an old contact, which is why I came to you.'

'Desperate measures, then?'

'How do I get to Jagger?'

'You're in luck, Snow. You're exactly his type.'

'Type?'

'He likes tall women with a bit of spirit about them. So go to the Korova nightclub tomorrow and use your charm on him.'

'Wouldn't it be easier to go to his house?'

Thorn laughed. 'The security at Jagger's mansion is presidential. So you won't get through that. No, the Korova is one of many properties he owns, and he spends more time there than anywhere else. So it's your best bet for having a conversation with him.'

'If he sent those thugs for me, won't he recognise me anyway in the nightclub?'

'Not if he's drunk enough. He does like a tipple. And even if he does, I'm sure you can handle yourself.'

'Even with this super security you mentioned?'

'He sends them away during his romantic liaisons. So you should be okay to extract the information you need.'

'You sound keen for me to go.'

Thorn shrugged. 'Not at all.' She pulled on the dog's lead. 'You came to me, remember?'

'I did, but I have the impression you want a favour from me in return.'

'Find his private laptop and copy as much data as possible. Then you might get enough for us to charge him and answer what happened to DC Ritchie.'

'And what if he refuses?'

Thorn allowed the dog to pull her away from Astrid.

'I've heard you're a woman of mass distraction, Snow. So use those skills to persuade him to talk.'

12 JULIA'S PUNISHMENT

Julia's punishment for breaking Paul's nose was swift. As he lay on the ground, mewling like a pig, the elders came for her. It wasn't the men who took her, but a group of women. She didn't protest as they dragged her away, feeling the pain in her knuckles from that punch.

She was like a rag doll in their hands, four women older than her, people she knew and was friendly with. But there was no friendship in their eyes then, only anger. Julia wondered if her action would hurt them, whether Wood and the other men would use it to justify harsh measures against the women in The Community.

They dug fingernails into her arms as they hauled her away. They took her to the far end of the compound, past the horses and the pigs, throwing her down. Her knees hit the dirt before her hands did, the earth staining her palms as drizzle fell from the dark above her.

The oldest woman in the group, Samantha, grabbed Julia's hair and dragged her across the ground, scraping the skin from her legs. Then the others joined in, holding Julia's arms and placing them on the stump used for chopping wood. Julia's malaise sped from her; twisting her neck around, she tried to wriggle from their grasp.

But it was no good.

She found her voice, screaming at them, begging for release.

Samantha approached Julia with an axe in her hands.

The other women pushed down hard on her arms, forcing her head forward so she was close to the wood. She couldn't see Samantha or the edge of the blade, but she heard her footsteps moving over the broken branches around them. Invisible fingers burrowed their way into Julia, gripping her heart and squeezing the life from her. She continued to struggle against her captors, but it was to no avail. She stopped shouting as she saw the moonlight reflected in the axe's blade, and silence surrounded her.

The air shivered as Samantha lifted the axe. Julia peered at her hands and knew what was coming.

Then the axe fell and she waited for the pain to shoot through her. The agony came not from the loss of a hand or fingers, but because the flat side of the blade crashed into her palm. Shards of electricity sped through Julia's hand and up her arm. She bit into her top lip as Samantha raised the blade again and brought it hard across her fingers. The action was repeated several times before she blacked out.

———

JULIA WAS INDOORS when she woke, lying on her bed as Samantha loomed over her.

'Your fingers are broken,' Samantha said. 'Paul wanted your hand chopped off, but Charles said no – we need you to work for The Community, and you can't do that with one hand.'

Julia felt nothing. She twisted off the bed and stared along her arm, peering at the bandages, but unable to move her fingers. Then she turned to Samantha.

'How many children have they taken from you?'

Blonde-haired blue-eyed Samantha was in her mid-forties, but could have been twenty years younger.

'The children of The Community are always with their parents wherever they go. We are all One with Him here.'

Julia swung her body around and stood on trembling legs.

'And who is that, the One and Him? Is that Charles or one of these aliens we're waiting for?'

'We all need guidance, Julia. No one person can navigate this life on their own. We need others for their support and love, and we have to provide support and love to others as well.'

Julia summoned all the strength she could to move her broken fingers, but the pain was so bad, she stopped, focusing on the older woman.

'I was born into this, Samantha; I had no choice. But you joined The Community, so what's your excuse?'

'I came here to escape everything I saw in the outside world: the misery wrought by greed; the poverty and war; the loneliness and the cruelty of it all. So I joined a commune: a community where people shared what little they had, spoke of love and peace; a world without money; who had a cause. A family. A community.'

Julia stared at her, understanding why someone would want to escape into a place where they felt safe and loved, yet unable to comprehend how Samantha thought she'd found that in The Community when there was evidence around her it was the complete opposite.

She held up her broken fingers. 'Isn't this cruelty?'

'Actions have consequences, Julia, and violent actions must be punished to maintain a civilised community. You broke Paul's nose, so your punishment had to be equal to what you did.'

'He wanted me to sleep with him.'

Samantha shook her head. 'Nobody is forced into anything here. You say no and walk away. You don't use violence on him.'

Julia laughed as her fingers ached.

'Is that what happens here? You refuse what a man wants, especially Paul or Charles, and your life goes on as normal? My baby was taken from me and I couldn't do anything about it.'

'Children belonging only to their birth parents is an evil of the outside world. It creates an environment fostered by jealousy and believing that your "blood family" is more important than anybody else. This leads to possessiveness, anger, and disappointment – all things that fuel violence and hate.'

Julia gazed into Samantha's eyes and knew she believed every word she'd said.

'So what happens to me now?'

'You can leave anytime you want, but there is no coming back once you abandon The Community. And you'll never see your child again.'

Julia's hand throbbed as if plugged into an electrical socket. She wanted to leave this place, but there was something she needed more: to find her daughter.

So she'd do anything to discover where Sophia was.

13   ASTRID VISITS A NIGHTCLUB

Astrid stood across from the Korova nightclub, staring at the sign hanging over the entrance of a woman bent into the shape of a table. The queue was long, so she waited for it to go down. As she did, Astrid returned to the information she'd found online about Paul Jagger: forty-two years old, born in Islington, single, formed his own fashion company when he was eighteen, which he sold for millions three years later. Then he went into property development, increasing his fortune as he made partnerships with influential middle-eastern individuals and American companies.

She peered at the photos, the hipster beard and the scars on his cheeks, examining the glint in his eyes. She was still looking at the screen when the limousine pulled up outside the nightclub. Two giants got out of the car, followed by Jagger dressed in a snazzy aquamarine suit and brilliant white shirt. The queue sank back before them as they entered the club.

Astrid took a deep breath. 'This better work.'

She crossed the road, pulling at the only skirt she could find in the minimum amount of clothes she had in the hotel.

It felt short to her as the hem rested on her knees, but she knew it was nothing compared to what the other women were wearing.

Astrid paid twenty quid to get in, already wondering if she'd have enough money in her account to last the night without going into the red. Lights sparkled above her head as she followed the other club-goers down the stairs and into the basement. It smelt of fresh flowers, even though she couldn't see any. She found multi-coloured leather chairs and sofas in the seating area, with space next to the bar for the DJ and a dancefloor.

She didn't know where Jagger and his goons had gone, so she went for a drink. Cider was way too downmarket for this venue to stock, so she spent £15 on a cocktail that looked like they'd emptied it from a hippopotamuses guts. Thankfully, it tasted a lot better than it appeared. She moved towards the far wall, scrutinising the other customers, wondering how she'd get Jagger to notice her amongst all the younger and more skimpily dressed women there.

A young bloke sidled up to Astrid, smiling through teeth that were so white, she assumed he must be American. She couldn't hear what he said to her over the noise of the music and didn't move to get any closer to him.

He spoke again. 'I like what you're wearing.'

It wasn't the worst chat-up line she'd ever received, but not only was he far too young for her, he was not her type. She was used to dealing with the unwanted attention of people, but it was in dive bars or down-at-heel pubs, not posh places like this.

She downed the rest of the cocktail and showed him the empty glass.

'I'll have another of these.'

He scuttled off to the bar as she scanned the surroundings again for Jagger, wondering if he'd gone off to one of the club's expensive tables: £1,000 to sit there for three hours and drink as much as you could.

She thought about that amount of money and the people who could fritter it away on nothing. The idea of it resurrected the image of Ramon ratting out his mates, and then skipping the country with the millions of pounds she'd stolen. However, she hadn't minded the online thieving, considering those she'd stolen from were even more corrupt than those she was associating with.

Ramon's glittering eyes lingered at the back of her memories as she glanced at the bloke holding her drink at the bar, watching as he removed something from his pocket and slipped it into the glass.

She blew out her cheeks, deliberating how to deal with the situation. By the time he returned to her, she knew there was only one thing she could do to stop him from doing this to other women.

Astrid took the glass from him, but didn't drink it. He was grinning at her when she saw Jagger reappear with his two goons. Then she grabbed the young bloke's free hand and dragged him towards the Korova's wealthy owner. She threw the bloke at the feet of the thugs and dumped her spiked booze all over him.

She scowled at Jagger as she stood between his security.

'This is some joint you run. This runt just put drugs into my drink, so what will you do about it?'

From the look in Jagger's glazed eyes, she guessed he'd already partaken of something more substantial than alcohol before he'd arrived. He peered at the bloke on the floor who was pleading his innocence before nodding to his goons. They grabbed the pervert and dragged him out through the back of the room.

'I'm sorry,' Jagger said. 'I promise you he won't do that ever again, in here or anywhere else. Can I get you a drink as a small token of my regret that you had to experience such a terrible thing in my club?'

'Champagne will do,' she said.

He waved a hand at the bar. 'Of course. I wouldn't have expected anything less from such exquisite beauty.' His teeth were porcelain white. 'Is this your first time here?'

'It is. And it will be the last at this rate.'

He laughed. 'Oh, we can't have that, can we?'

She smiled as she let him lead her away from the rest of the crowd towards a set of tables in the far corner. A young woman brought the champagne and two glasses as they sat. Astrid watched him pouring the drinks, scrutinising his face to see if he recognised her or not.

He handed her the drink. 'I'm Paul Jagger.'

She sipped at the bubbles in her glass. 'A man of wealth and taste.'

His grin was brighter than the lights sparkling above their heads.

'You've heard of me, then?'

'You don't recognise the words?'

The dark confusion on his face mixed in with the shadows at their feet. 'What?'

'You're not a big Stones fan, I gather.'

He choked on his champagne. 'That's way before my time. This is more my kind of music.' He held up one hand to the dance tune blaring through the speakers.

She scanned the rest of the room, searching for his security and finding them easily enough: at the bar trying to mix in with the youthful customers, looking as out of place as a piece of steak at a vegetarian banquet.

'You're right; this is a good tune,' she said. 'I think I know this band; aren't they called Scorpio or something like that?'

He shrugged and drank more. 'Don't know and don't care. Do you want to dance?'

It was the last thing she wanted to do. So instead, she stretched out her leg and showed him a bit of thigh and the shoes she was wearing: the ones she'd bought from a charity shop close to her hotel earlier in the day.

'I'd love to dance, but I can't in these heels.' She glanced at the dancefloor. 'I'd go barefoot, but I don't trust that surface and the people on it.'

Jagger never took his eyes off her legs as she was talking. Then he leant into her.

'You know, I have a private dancefloor and enough champagne to last the rest of the night back at my place.'

Astrid studied his face, recognised the drugs shimmering there and thought how this was going to be a lot easier than she'd expected.

'What about food? I haven't eaten all day.'

At least that wasn't a lie.

The glimmer from the disco lights created a halo behind his head.

'The kitchen is well-stocked, or I can send one of my security out for a takeaway. Whatever you want.'

Astrid agreed as her stomach rumbled. They finished the drinks, and then Jagger led her out of the club, the crowd parting before them as if he was Moses approaching the Red Sea. Outside, she got into the back of the limo, sinking into its luxurious interior. Before the car had set off, the multi-millionaire was cracking open another bottle of champagne.

She took the glass from him, returning his smile as her mind unwrapped several escape maps for her upcoming situation. Once she'd accepted Thorn's suggestion of visiting the Korova nightclub, Astrid had done her due diligence of online research for Jagger's London mansion. She knew it had four floors, including a basement, five bedrooms, six bathrooms, a private gym, cinema room, three double garages and a spa. She'd memorised all points of entry and exit while realising the internal security was extensive, regardless of what Thorn had said about Jagger's goons leaving him alone while he entertained his female guests.

But she pushed the escape maps to the back of her mind, focused on how she'd make him tell her what he knew about Courtney and Olivia.

That's if he was the mysterious Scorpio.

The car jerked forward as she laughed and sipped at the bubbles. Jagger forced his leg next to hers, his hand drifting over her knee as he bragged about how successful his latest property development had been. She nodded and agreed with how wonderful he was.

The driver turned the music up – KC and the Sunshine Band on their eternal celebration – as they downed their drinks and she thought ahead of how she'd get out of the mansion unscathed.

Thirty minutes later, they'd finished the bottle of fizz as they drove through acres of private land and pulled up outside the mansion. Parked near the property were a Rolls Royce and Ferrari. Astrid staggered out of the car, her unsteadiness more to do with her high heels than what she'd drunk. Jagger moved ahead of her, over a rocky driveway and towards the steps leading up to the impressive building. Two of his goons were on either side of them until one broke away to open the front door.

They entered a large hall with pristine wooden flooring, a single luxurious chair, and a marble staircase. Jagger's security disappeared as he grabbed Astrid's hand. She thought he was going to attempt to take her straight to a bedroom; instead, he led her through a door and downstairs, where he switched a light on, and she gazed over an impressive collection of cars and motorbikes. His smile was one of a man happy in his world and even happier to show it to her.

Astrid went to the vehicles, running her hand over the Bugatti, Aston Martin, and Porsche, noticing that gleam in his eyes and recognising it as him imaging his hands on her. But she wasn't interested in the cars, glancing at the motorbikes to ensure the keys were in the machines. Then she located the switch to open the garage and knew how she'd get out of the building.

All she had to do was get the information she needed from him.

Jagger grinned at her. 'Perhaps we can take one of these out for a spin tomorrow morning.'

His confidence that she'd be staying the night pleased Astrid; she knew it would be his undoing.

'How about that food you mentioned? How close is the nearest Indian restaurant?'

'A curry? I admire a woman who likes it spicy.' He removed a mobile phone from his jacket. 'Tell me what you want, and I'll send one of my men for it. It will be quicker than having to wait for a delivery, about forty minutes.' Jagger beamed at her. 'Plenty of time for us to get to know each other better.'

'What about your other security guards?' she said.

'Oh, don't worry about them. They stay in the cottage at the end of the drive when I'm home.'

'Great. I'll have a chicken Rogan Josh, egg rice, and a garlic naan bread.'

He nodded before speaking into the phone. Then he slipped the mobile into his pocket.

'All done. Would you like to see the rest of the house?'

'Of course.'

Especially wherever you've got your computer.

Jagger took her back upstairs, through the impressive hall and into a kitchen bigger than most houses Astrid had lived in. The walls were a brilliant white and matched the large table in the middle of the room. She watched him as he went to the fridge and removed a bottle of champagne. The glasses were behind her and she got two, her top lip curling upwards as he filled them with fizz and handed her one. She lifted it to her mouth, sipping on the bubbles and gazing into his eyes. From an early age, she'd always been good at not letting alcohol affect her too much as long as she didn't mix her drinks, which was why she was still feeling okay, though he appeared to be flusher in the face than when she'd first seen him in the nightclub.

'I'll get the plates and cutlery ready,' he said as he went to a cupboard.

Astrid placed her glass on the table and moved towards the window, peering at the countryside. Shimmering yellow and blue lights surrounded the steam coming off a Jacuzzi, and she speculated on how long it would take him to suggest they retire into that hot water.

She turned back to see him holding their drinks.

'Time for the living room,' she said.

Jagger handed Astrid her champagne and led her into

the main room. She didn't see a TV or any computers, only two huge sofas, shelves filled with objects of art, and a piano and stool near the large window that looked out into the vast garden.

He removed his jacket and threw it over the sofa. She knew he was ready to make his move.

But so was she.

And that's when she blacked out.

The inside of Astrid's head felt like it was underwater, with a torrent pushing her brain against her skull. Her eyelids were heavier than lead when she got them open and peered blurry-eyed at Jagger sitting opposite her. He was cross-legged on a comfy sofa, but her arms were tied onto a rickety chair. The room smelt of curry as she watched him chew on a piece of naan bread.

'I hope you don't mind, Astrid, but I started without you.'

She rolled her tongue around, still tasting the champagne, but now noticing there was something else underneath the pop of the bubbles.

'You drugged me.'

Stupid and lazy.

Curry slipped over the top of his lip. 'I had no choice.'

She tasted blood in the far corner of her mouth.

'Do you do this to many women? You're no better than the other bloke I caught spiking my drink in your nightclub.'

He shook his head. 'It's got nothing to do with that.'

A giant concrete ball bounced off the sides of her skull.

'Is this because of yesterday?'

He licked the sauce off his chin. 'I don't know what you're talking about, Ms Snow.'

She flexed her arms against the restraints, but with no luck. At least her legs were free.

'There's no need to lie to me now, Scorpio. I wouldn't go with your goons to the pub, and this is how you get back at women who refuse your advances.'

He laughed in her face. 'Women never refuse me, Astrid. Not if they want to live long.' He stopped eating and uncrossed his legs. 'Why did you call me Scorpio?'

'You're not Scorpio, the mysterious leader of a people-trafficking gang who sent two goons after me?'

Jagger grinned. 'Unfortunately not, since he sounds like a wonderful bloke.'

'So, how do you know who I am?'

He wiped curry from his fingers over his expensive trousers and reached down to his feet to get a laptop. He opened it and showed her the images on the screen: video frames of Astrid entering the Korova nightclub.

'For security, my people film everybody who enters my premises. Then they search online to discover who they are and if they pose any threat to my organisation or me. It's easy when people pay with credit cards, which is the majority now. But a few still use cash, and we use facial recognition software with them.'

'Where did you get that? It's only available to the security services and the police.'

'My organisation has many influential contacts, Astrid.'

'Would that be your crime empire or the façade you show the world?'

He beamed at her. 'Both. Do you know what they

discovered when my highly skilled digital team searched for you?'

'That I was the school chess champion when girls weren't allowed to play the game?'

He leant closer to her. 'They found only one thing: a video clip of you entering a building two days ago. This wasn't on the internet, but in the data we store from various secret cameras across the city. Can you guess which building it was?'

It could only be one. 'The police station.'

Jagger pressed his knees into hers.

'Indeed. So there I am in the Korova when this mysterious, beautiful woman appears. Then she throws a pervert at my feet as a gamble to get my attention.' He laughed again. 'That was a good move, by the way. And while you were talking to me, my people were providing information through the communicator in my ear; all passed on by a contact I have at Kentish Town police station.' He placed dirty fingers on her knee and gripped hard. 'There was you gabbing away at me in the nightclub, and all the while, I'm hearing about Astrid Snow and her missing sister.' She smelt the curry coming off him. 'A delightful tale of how your sister hates you because, a long time ago, you told your father's employers – the police, ironically enough – that he was beating you every day. So they locked him up, and you ran away, turning up a few years later with a bunch of street thugs before you disappeared again. It was such a fascinating story, and I was so looking forward to you telling me more about your colourful life.' He continued to squeeze her leg. 'But alas, you're employed by the coppers as another of their undercover floozies trying to bring me down.'

She ignored her pain. 'You're not Scorpio and you didn't send two goons to get me yesterday?'

'That's nothing to do with me.' He had his hands on both knees, pushing them apart so he could place his legs between hers. 'Are you going to tell me why you agreed to work for the pigs, especially considering what your old man did to you?'

'Have the police done that to you before?'

His breath was hot on her face. 'Sent women undercover to spy on me? On more than one occasion, but we always catch them in the end. You were the quickest of the bunch.'

She smiled at him. 'You might as well ease your guilty conscience, Paul, and tell me everything now.'

'Did the coppers put a recording device on you, Astrid?'

He stood, placed his hands on her shoulders before removing her jacket and dropping it next to her bag. She knew what was coming, but still shivered when he reached inside her top and his cold fingers crawled over her skin.

'Is this how you get your kicks, Paul, molesting helpless women?'

His nails cut into her flesh as he moved his hands to her back, then over Astrid's stomach, before resting on her bra. He stank of curry and sweat, and she had to resist the temptation to spit in his face.

Jagger left his grubby fingers lingering on her. 'I doubt you've ever been helpless, Astrid, not since you dobbed your old man in to the coppers.' He removed his hands from under her top. 'It will be easier if I just take your skirt off, don't you think?'

He got off her, looming over her like a dark shadow.

But her legs were free.

So she jerked up and kicked him in the balls.

He stumbled into the sofa, crying out as his face resembled a squashed orange. As he crashed into the furniture,

Astrid stood and threw her back onto the ground. The flimsy chair snapped into pieces as she hit the wood beneath her. Agony shot through her bones as she rolled on her side and wriggled her hands free. But before she could get up, he was on top of her with his fingers around her throat.

'I'm going to enjoy this,' he said as his knee dug into her spine.

His weight pushed her face into the floor, her nose pressed against the wood as she struggled to breathe. Jagger's fingernails drew blood as he forced his face into her neck.

She snapped her head back, her skull connecting with his chin as he pulled her up, and they stumbled around the room like he was riding a wild stallion, and she was the horse.

They hit a table first, the leg cracking into her knee as she flailed to shake him off. Then they staggered forward, Astrid hitting the piano and falling over it, her head playing manic music on the keys as he dragged her across the ivory. He kept on pushing her down, the screeching from the piano assaulting her ears and tearing at her skin.

She reached down, scrambling for a weapon and finding pieces of the chair. Astrid grabbed a bit and stabbed his leg. He screamed as he pulled her back with him. Falling into the shelves and taking expensive ornaments down with them, they rolled over broken ceramic, bits of it digging into her legs as she got his fingers off her throat. His eyes were blood-red as he roared at her.

Then Astrid kicked him in the balls again.

He grabbed at his groin as his face twisted in agony. She jumped up and scanned the doors, expecting to see his security burst in at any second. When they didn't, she seized him by the shirt and dragged him across the room, Jagger spitting blood over the damage they'd caused. She dumped him at the foot of the sofa, wiped at the bruise on her neck, and retrieved his laptop. Then she got her bag and removed a USB stick from it.

'What are you doing?' he snarled.

She ignored him and plugged the device into the computer. Then Astrid rested it in her lap as she sat, searching through his files while keeping one eye on him.

'Are you rash enough to keep records of your people trafficking on here?'

He wiped snot from his nose over his sleeve.

'There is no people trafficking, you stupid mare, not from my organisation. I don't get involved in grubby stuff like that. It's the Eastern European gangs who make their money that way.'

She let him ramble on while she searched the laptop, frustrated but not surprised at finding nothing criminal.

Should I ask him about the missing police officer, DC June Ritchie?

She found a folder of videos and photographs organised under female names. There wasn't one for Ritchie, but she glanced through the first few, grimacing at what she saw. She turned the computer towards him and played a video on the list.

'What happened to Ashley after you filmed this, Paul?'

In the clip, Ashley's screams sent a shiver down Astrid's back, but she didn't stop it.

'It's consensual. They all signed a contract before I did anything to them.'

Astrid stopped the video and copied everything in that folder to the USB drive.

'What do you know about the disappearance of my sister Courtney and her daughter Olivia?'

He shook his head. 'I told you, nothing. I'd never heard of you or them until you came into my club. So I'm not this Scorpio you're after.'

She removed the USB drive when all the files were copied.

'You've never heard of Mr Scorpio? So he's not one of your criminal competitors?'

'No. That name means nothing to me.'

Astrid peered into his pained eyes, knowing he'd told the truth. She put the drive into her bag. There was no need for her to linger there any longer.

Then the two security goons came in. She only glanced at them.

'Tell them to leave, Jagger.'

He laughed at her. 'I'm going to let them play with you before I have a go and add you to my video collection, Snow.'

The gorillas moved into the room, striding towards her with menace. Jagger's twisted smile was wide enough to cover his face. She put her foot on his injured leg and pressed down.

He screamed and the men stopped, unsure what to do.

Jagger's face contorted into something barely human. 'Kill the bitch!'

They ran at her together, but their bulk and the lack of space limited their speed, allowing her the time to grab Jagger and hurl him at them. He hit them, taking all three into and over a coffee table. She left them swearing in a heap and sprinted out of the room.

She reached the doorway to the garage as the quicker of the goons grabbed her shoulder. She twisted to shake him off, but all she did was take the two of them tumbling down the stairs. They bounced off them like entwined lovers. Her back smacked into the steps as he dug his fingers into her arms. Pain surged through every inch of her as she bit into her lip and tasted blood. Astrid was underneath him, taking most of the bumps as they rolled into the garage and the wheels of the nearest car.

She wriggled away from him and jumped up, expecting another attack, but he was out cold. Astrid checked he was alive before grabbing her bag, making sure the USB drive was there, then running to the closest motorbike. She was sitting on it with the keys in her hand when Jagger and the other goon appeared.

'Don't make this harder than it needs to be, Paul,' she said.

His swagger had returned with the paid muscle by his side.

'Give me that USB drive and we might let you live.'

She put the keys into the ignition and turned it on. She looked at the security guy.

'Open the garage door and I won't hurt you.'

He glanced at her, then at his boss before doing as she said. Astrid nodded at him as she drove out of the building. She wasn't dressed or wearing the right shoes for riding a motorbike, but she increased the speed and headed out of the grounds.

The wind whipped through her hair and every muscle ached in her body.

And she was still no further forward in finding Courtney and Olivia.

15   JULIA'S ESCAPE

While her broken fingers healed, Julia worked in The Community's school. She couldn't play the guitar anymore, but she could help the kids. On her first day there, the sun was shining, everywhere smelt of fresh flowers, and the birds serenaded her journey to the school. The pain was subdued in her hand as she heard the bell ringing. Groups of children, some of them barefoot, scampered around her while the youngest were pushed past her in wooden carts.

All the adults were smiling while collecting washing for the communal laundry, dealing with the animals, or working on the crops. They shared the work and reaped the benefits, living as one group, happy with everything they did. Yet she watched them through new eyes, clearly understanding this community wasn't for her.

But she couldn't leave.

Not until she knew where Sophia was. And Julia would use her new job to help her get what she wanted.

She didn't know if the elders had registered the school with the local council – they were living on a large plot of land outside Glasgow. Still, she didn't care as it allowed her access to things unavailable to her before, including a mobile and the internet.

Julia had to return the phone to Samantha after every lesson, but she had it for two hours before each class to prepare for the teaching. So as long as she erased the browsing history before handing it back, she thought she'd be okay.

And she enjoyed working with the kids. Assisting the teachers in the classes became more than a distraction for her as the experience created something in her she hadn't had before: a true sense of purpose. She knew helping others through education was what she'd do once she left The Community. But she couldn't do that until she completed the most important thing in her life – finding Sophia.

Yet it didn't take long for her to realise how hopeless it was trying to find her parents. Putting their names into a search returned no useful results. Even when she searched for The Community, she was surprised at how few results she got, none of which mentioned what went on inside the group.

But what she found was people saying The Community was a cult.

A cult.

She hadn't known what the term meant until those internet search results.

Was The Community a cult?

What was the difference between living and working together to achieve well-being and a fully fledged cult?

That question possessed her mind as she read all the articles until her brain hurt. Still, one conclusion stood out more to her than the others: coercive control manifested itself in different circumstances – within cults, in trafficking environments, and intimate partner violence. The more she delved into this, the more she agreed with it. Her parents and Samantha – and all the other adults – had been coerced to join The Community by Wood, and then manipulated to stay and go along with actions most people would perceive as wrong. Her parents had trafficked Julia, and then Sophia into an organisation that would use them for their benefit. And the more time she spent around Samantha and the other women, the more she recognised how many had been groomed – whether it was grooming to join or stay in the group or to accept subservience and involvement in unwanted relationships and sex.

This was when she understood why Wood was using the idea of aliens coming to save The Community from the dire consequences of climate change. Charles Wood's agenda was about creating fear from an apparent apocalyptic event while proclaiming himself as the saviour.

With every moment she spent there, this became clearer to Julia – but it wasn't to anybody else. So she never broached the subject with the others, never asked if they believed the alien story was real for fear of people reporting her to Wood or the other elders. It didn't take long for her to realise she couldn't change the minds of those around her – all she could do was get away from them and find Sophia.

Samantha had told Julia she could leave The Community, but she wouldn't put that promise to the test by telling the elders she was going. It was painful for her to abandon the children, guilt weighing on her in the knowledge of the life they had ahead of them – already two of the sixteen-year-old girls were pregnant – but she had no choice but to leave them behind.

Julia waited until three in the morning, slipping out of the house through the rear door. She stuck to the shadows as she went, never looking back as she strode past the spot where Samantha had broken her fingers. The nearest town was two hours from the compound. For all of that journey, she expected a hand on her shoulder; an elder to tell her it had all been a joke and she'd have to live with them forever. The only thing that kept her going, that forced her legs to move through the cold and the damp, was the thought of finding her daughter.

That was the first promise she made to herself: that she'd never leave Sophia again once she found her.

The second promise was to help others, those forced into lives that were painful for them. She couldn't end the suffering of the children she'd abandoned in The Community, but – from this point on – she'd do everything in her power to help others.

The early morning sun caressed Astrid's face as she drove from Jagger's mansion, heading not to her hotel, but her sister's place. It wasn't because she was worried he or his goons would follow her, but after coming away empty-handed in the search for Courtney and Olivia, she was desperate to go over the ground she'd already covered. So first, she'd try Courtney's house, and then Vanessa Moore's flat. If she had no leads after that, she'd have to return to the police.

Thorn knows more than she's letting on – I'm sure about that.

She parked the motorbike around the corner from the house, just in case Jagger might be stupid enough to report it stolen. Which it was. She touched the USB drive in her pocket, wondering if he was telling the truth about those videos. What she'd witnessed wasn't mild sex games with a bit of S&M involved – it was sexual sadism taken to the limit. Mild sadists seek masochistic partners, and their behaviours are consensual. Major sadism, however, isn't consensual and can involve injury and death. The sadist desires complete control and compliance, wanting their victim to feel fear. It's this fear that turns them on. And she'd seen that in Jagger on those videos. So even when she had him helpless before her, she knew he was enjoying the fact she'd had to watch those clips.

Astrid had encountered extreme sexual sadists before. They were predominately male, but she'd met plenty of women who enjoyed the world of sadomasochistic sex, and she still had contacts in the dominatrix community.

Perhaps I should speak to one of them about Jagger.

She pushed that thought from her head and focused on her sister and niece. She went to the back of the house, taking the key from the box. When she opened the door and stepped into the kitchen, she knew someone else had been there since her last visit. Certain things were in different places now – the kettle had been moved, a tap was dripping, and there were marks on the floor which weren't there before.

Astrid assumed it must have been the police as she went into the living room. It appeared untouched as she set about searching the house again, hoping to discover something she might have missed.

It took her thirty minutes to find it. Returning to the bloodstain in the bedroom, she kicked herself for not noticing it before – the carpet was damaged close to the stain and near the bed. Astrid bent her legs and pulled at it, taking it back until she saw the floorboards. The blood hadn't seeped through to the wood, but she found something more interesting – a gap where she could get her fingers inside and prise the floor up.

She took a deep breath when she found the envelope. Dust covered it, and a spider scuttled out of the corner as she grabbed the paper. Would this be just another page of cryptic text like she'd found last time, that piece with the words VAN and GUARD on it?

Astrid grabbed the envelope and sat on the bed. Then she opened it and removed the contents: three A4 pages of neat handwriting. She read them more than once.

DEAR VANESSA

I was a stranger in a strange land until I met you. You told me it would help me to write about my life, so I've sent this to you, my saviour.

'Go back home.'

That's what people said to me, words thrown at me like bricks.

'Go back home. You don't belong here.'

But all my homes no longer existed. Instead, the buses zigzagging around the city were my transitory houses, temporary communities of the lonely and the destitute marked out as someone to be avoided, to be shunned.

I was a stranger in a strange land.

Wintertime was the worst. The wind would cut across my face, dredging up memories of being hauled from my bed and forced to watch my parents dragged away. The cold would rush up my legs, seeking shelter underneath clothes scavenged from bins and dumpsters. The only warmth I found was with others like me, shivering around the fires we built away from civilised people.

The flames would reignite memories of a different version of me: a younger, happier one, sitting next to an electric fire in our home. My father would cook, the smell of fried meat and vegetables alien to the strange land where I'd end up. But one day, uniformed men barged into our house and dragged my parents away, calling them traitors and rebels.

They didn't protest; to protest would make it worse. I never saw them again except inside my head. That was the first time I lost my home. It wouldn't be the last.

'Go back home.' Sometimes followed by 'You don't belong here.'

That's what people said to me.

There were others like me in our village and I hid with them in the forest. Food was scarce, so we ate from the land: berries and mushrooms. We'd catch rats, but there wasn't much meat on them. I had no time to think about what I'd lost or focus on my parents' fate. So when we weren't struggling to survive, we were hiding from those searching for us, constantly moving and in fear for our lives.

I don't know how long that lasted, but it was soon after my fifteenth birthday when a man said he could get me and others out of the country. He led us out of the forest and into the nearest town. At first, I was scared he was taking us to the men who'd dragged my parents away, but I knew I had no other choices left to me. Smoke filled the air from where the bombs had dropped, destroying every building I could see — the destruction was never-ending, stretching from one end of the horizon to the other. All around me were the dead; people with no hands, no arms, or no legs. There were a dozen of us stumbling through this landscape, women or children like me — some of them even younger — and all we could do was look on and cry.

Once, we had to hide on a mountain because there was a battle nearby between two groups. I didn't know who they were or what they were fighting for. The man helping us kept us safe in a barn, providing food and water. He said we'd be okay once we were out of the country. None of us asked him where we were going or what we'd do when we got there. We just wanted to escape.

I was scared all the time, hearing the bombs and gunshots near where we were. It was difficult to sleep, but when I did, I'd always jump awake at the slightest noise, expecting the men to come in and drag me away. We had to hide in that barn for five days, only leaving when the food and water ran out. One woman died next to me in the middle of the night.

Eventually, the man took us out, and a truck was waiting for us. We all huddled into the back underneath dirty, wet covers, struggling to stay warm as rockets lit up the sky. We travelled overland for days, never stopping, rarely eating or drinking, and having to go to the toilet where we lay. By the time we reached the sea, I was filthy and desperate for water. The man had others with him then, and they gave us food and drink before taking us aboard a boat. He led us below, saying our journey was nearly over. We shivered in the dark and the damp for ages. Several children were sick because of the movement over the water, but I ate little, letting the knot in my stomach grow until the pain became too unbearable and I passed out.

When I woke, a woman was helping me off the boat. We were on dry land again, but there were no sounds of explosions or guns; only the birds singing and the sun on my face. She helped me into the back of a truck with the others. As I settled into the rear, I counted how many were left – eight from the original twelve. But there were newcomers with us, more women and children. The only men I saw were the ones helping us.

I expected to be in that truck for days, but it wasn't long before we arrived in a big city and the men took us out. There was no destruction around me, no death and despair, just the tallest buildings I'd ever seen. I smiled when I saw them, but it was the last smile I'd have until I met you, Vanessa.

The original man who helped us out of the forest had vanished, replaced by others with dark eyes and stern faces. They provided new clothes and access to showers, but it wasn't out of the goodness of their hearts. We were to work for them, to pay off the debt we owed.

Now I had a second home. They forced me to work in a factory, putting things into boxes and bottles, and the owners provided beds for all the workers. I suppose it wasn't home, but it was something. It could have been worse. It was worse for many others – I heard the stories of what women and girls were made to do. At least I was safe from that. The days were long and hard, but I was alive. We were never allowed out of the factory or the tiny rooms where they kept us.

Then one day, the factory burned to the ground and twelve people died. The authorities never investigated, but accusing fingers pointed at the strangers; at those like me. So I ran away.

'Go back home.'

'You don't belong here.'

'Go back home.'

A stranger in a strange land.

I trawled the streets, eating rats again, finding shelter in doorways or under bridges. And then I met others like me: girls and young women with nowhere to live and no prospects of a normal life.

That was until the men came, offering drugs and clothes, saying they'd look after us. So I was fed and clothed, and I felt safe.

But only for a little while.

The men said I owed them thousands of pounds, and there was only one way to pay it back. They took me to different houses, into dirty rooms where smelly men waited for me, dozens of them every day. I said no, but they beat me. I wanted to die. I was lost.

But then you found me, Vanessa.

My angel.

My saviour.

You can destroy this when you've read it because that part of my life is over.

Now I'm normal again.

And it's all because of you.

Love.

Zoe.

ASTRID SAT in silence after the second reading, peering at the letters on the pages as if she was connected to the young woman who'd written them.

This confirmed Vanessa Moore had assisted trafficked girls and women to escape from their captors.

But where was Moore now?

And was Courtney involved in helping the victims?

17 ASTRID MAKES A FRIEND

Astrid didn't need to break into Moore's flat this time as the door was open when she got there. She stepped inside, expecting the police or the neighbour, surprised instead to see a distinctive flame-haired woman sitting on the floor going through the box of photos.

She glanced up as Astrid entered, a woman as tall as her, wearing brilliant white training shoes with leather trousers and a jacket that were as red as her hair. When she smiled at Astrid, the dimple in her chin appeared to move as her lips did.

'Ah, Snow. You saved me the trip of having to find you.'

The woman didn't shift from the floor, staying cross-legged with piles of photographs spread near her.

'Who are you?' Astrid said.

'I have many names,' she replied, 'but you can call me Ophelia Red.' She pulled at a strand of her long, curly hair. 'It suits my current appearance, don't you think?'

Astrid glanced around the room to see if anybody else was there.

'Do you know where Vanessa Moore is?'

Ophelia Red smiled at her. 'Ms Moore appears to have vanished, just like several women and girls across the city.' She lifted one photo from the pile, a picture of a dark-haired woman. 'I'm looking for somebody as well, just like you are. Perhaps we can work together.'

Astrid gazed at her. 'Who sent you here? Was it Jagger?'

Ophelia shook her head. 'I'm a private contractor; I'm sure you know how that works. I'm not at liberty to say who hired me, only that our interests appear to be merging.'

'Who are you looking for?' Astrid said.

Ophelia dropped the picture into the pile and stood. Then she removed a snap of a smiling blue-eyed teenage girl from her pocket.

'This is Kate Gregory. Do you know her or where she is?'

Astrid glanced at the photo, noticing the marks on the other woman's fingers.

'Never seen her before. Who is she to you?'

'That doesn't matter,' Ophelia said. 'She's fifteen and missing, and I've been tasked with finding her.'

'What brought you here?' Astrid said.

Ophelia returned the image to her pocket. 'My sources told me Moore has been helping trafficked women and girls get out of the country. So I came here to speak to her.' She held up her hands. 'Alas, the next-door neighbour informed me Vanessa is missing. But I learned from Moore's colleagues at work she's good friends with your sister, Courtney. So she was to be my next port of call until I learned from the police she's also disappeared.' She glanced at the images at her feet. 'This is not a good sign, is it, Astrid?'

Astrid's irritation that certain people knew more about her than she did about them grew by the second.

'How do you know who I am?'

Ophelia shrugged. 'It's what I do, Ms Snow. Of course, I'm not as experienced as you at this – I am younger, but I get by.'

'What do you mean by that?'

She flopped onto the sofa. 'Okay, I guess I need to share some things with you if we're going to create trust between us before we work together. I told you I'm a contractor – you know what that means?'

Astrid nodded. 'You go where the money is, working for anyone, regardless of morality and legality, to do the things normal people aren't supposed to do.'

Ophelia grinned. 'A bit like you, then?'

'No,' Astrid said. 'I'd never work for human scum like Paul Jagger.'

'Did morality play its part when you worked for the Agency, Astrid?'

Astrid took the seat opposite her, unsure how to handle this woman, but knowing she must be dangerous if she knew about the Agency.

'You don't work for them, not officially – you're too headstrong for the Agency to tolerate for too long – but you've freelanced for them, haven't you? Is that where you heard about me?'

Ophelia's grin grew bigger. 'You're a legend there, Astrid. I know they'd have you back in a heartbeat.' She moved forward a little. 'Though my understanding of the Agency is that their employees are there for life – only death, imprisonment or a complete mental collapse will get you out of their clutches. And even with the last option, you're likely still to be locked up somewhere the light rarely shines. So how did you get away from them?'

Astrid laughed. 'You expect me to work with you?'

Ophelia shrugged. 'Why not? We're both searching for missing people, and it seems obvious to me, as I'm sure it does to you, that one or more of London's trafficking gangs are involved somehow.'

'Tell me who it was that gave you this address?'

The redheaded woman played with a lock of hair as if she was a child about to reveal some scandalous secret.

'I have contacts in the police and the National Crime Agency, both of whom led me here. I thought Kate's photo might be in Moore's collection, but it isn't.' She gazed at Astrid. 'How is your sister involved in all this?'

Astrid was considering leaving – ignoring the woman and her question – until she thought this might be the only lead she'd get.

And she also had to admit Ophelia Red intrigued her.

Is it only intrigue or something more?

'They're teachers at the same school and, I assume, friends. I'm guessing Moore got involved in helping trafficked women and girls somehow, and then Courtney helped her.'

'You don't sound too convinced by that last bit.'

Astrid shook her head. 'The idea of my sister helping anybody, let alone victims of human trafficking, is hard to believe.'

'Is that because of what she did to you when you were kids?'

Astrid dug her nails into the sofa. 'Courtney did nothing to me.'

'Of course,' Ophelia said. 'She only encouraged your father's abuse and enjoyed watching you suffer.' Her smile had disappeared. 'I've read the evidence you gave at his trial.' She shook her head. 'That was shocking, and I feel for you, Astrid.'

Astrid glared at her. 'I don't need your sympathies. Tell me who Kate Gregory is to you, or I'm leaving.'

Ophelia's grin returned. 'What if I tried to stop you?'

Astrid's glare transformed into a smile.

'Now that would be fun.'

Ophelia ran her fingers through that flame-red hair again as she laughed.

'I'm sure it would, but maybe later. I'll tell you about Kate, but you need some backstory first.' She leant in closer to Astrid. 'How many successful romantic relationships have you had in your life, Astrid?'

Astrid settled into the sofa, more relaxed than she'd thought she'd be since her niece was still missing.

'Love is a mutually agreed-upon delusion.'

Ophelia rubbed at the marks on her fingers. 'Indeed, but it's a delusion we seek regardless of what it will do to us in the end, wouldn't you say?'

'That and a bottle of wine will get you through the night.'

'I'm more of a gin and tonic person myself. But I'm curious what you think of the changing nature of the male-female dynamic in the modern world compared to what women of previous generations had to endure.'

Astrid stretched her legs so her feet were near the photos.

'My interest in male-female relationships ended a long time ago.'

Ophelia beamed at her. 'Excellent. I knew you were a woman with impeccable taste. But this relates to Kate Gregory's mother, Allison, and the man she found herself in a relationship with after Kate's father died. It's an interesting perspective, this, and backs up a few thoughts I've had on the changing nature of relationships, especially between the fifties and the present day.' She was close enough for Astrid to smell the rose blossom in that distinctive hair. 'Do you think societal norms in the past encouraged women to settle for men they wouldn't normally have done, and that those norms, for a variety of reasons, don't exist anymore?'

Astrid stared at her, wondering when was the last time she'd had an interesting conversation with anyone that hadn't involved sex or booze.

'I could never comprehend why my mother ended up with Lawrence.'

'Your father?'

Astrid nodded. 'I don't think of him that way. Of course, I try not to think of him at all, but it's as Lawrence when I do.'

'I understand,' Ophelia said. 'My mother was much like Allison Gregory. My father was a terrible man, one of many terrible men I've met during my life. I'm talking about the dull and charmless blokes called Norman, Malcolm or Derek, all with less physical attractiveness than a showroom dummy: tank-top, comb-over, ill-advised moustache, wearing second-hand clothes and condemned to dead-end jobs. They were taciturn and stoic, often uncommunicative with a nasal drone, and always complained about how hard done by they'd been in life.

'Their hobbies usually involved being alone in a shed for long periods, while they were incredibly proud of minor achievements and advancements at work. They made Alan Partridge seem like a catch.

'Once upon a time, back in the dim and distant past, thanks to arcane mortgage regulations and sexist workplace culture, to achieve that sense of suburban stability and the whole two-point-four kids semi-detached milieu, many women would have to accept marrying a man like that. They'd put up with his numerous grating foibles in return for his reliable provision of a middle-management salary and genuine commitment to a stable family home life. I have no doubt the increase in divorce rates in the 80s and 90s was down to many early baby-boomer women, kids grown up and left, realising with horror they were about to enter middle age shackled to an Alan Partridge.'

Astrid smiled at her. 'You seem to have put a lot of thought into this.'

Ophelia laughed. 'I've had plenty of online conversations on this subject. It can get very lonely, being constantly stuck in a different hotel room in a different part of the country, don't you think?'

Astrid didn't answer the question. 'You're saying Kate Gregory's gone missing to get away from her mother's latest bloke, one of these types of men you're talking about?'

'Women no longer have to put up with charmless blokes anymore. They're no longer financially or socially dependent on that kind of partnership to buy a house or make ends meet, so relationships are about who's best rather than who'll do. So you would think it would also mean they could walk away from these unsatisfactory relationships and continue their lives without such baggage. But, unfortunately, for many men, this rejection is a great body blow to their self-esteem, and they feel the need to strike back at the women who've left them – and even to hurt their children.'

She took a deep breath, and Astrid didn't know if she was still talking about Kate Gregory's situation or her own.

'Who hired you to find Kate?'

'Allison Gregory is Paul Jagger's step-sister, from the family he abandoned when he made his fortune. She's also an old school friend of mine. I met her again recently through social media, and she told me Kate vanished two months ago. The police had done nothing, even when Allison told them she thinks Kate went to see Jagger at one of his nightclubs.'

Astrid thought about the USB drive in her pocket, knowing she'd have to check every video on there.

'Have you spoken to Jagger?'

'Not yet. My information is that, even though his crime organisation covers the city and other parts of the country, he doesn't get involved in what he sees as the dirty side of the business – the drugs, prostitution and trafficking. Instead, he prefers his corruption to come through dodgy business deals, tax fraud, and bent government contracts.'

Astrid scrutinised her face, unsure if she believed all she was hearing.

'What about Allison Gregory's boyfriend? If Kate was desperate to get away from him, he might have something to do with her disappearance.'

'He's dead,' Ophelia said. 'Found floating in the Thames two weeks ago with a single blow to the back of his head.'

'Was that your doing?'

Laughter burst out of her. 'My, Ms Snow, what do you take me for?'

'Do you have any leads on where Kate might be?'

Ophelia reached into her jacket and removed a small card. She handed it to Astrid.

'My contact at the National Crime Agency gave me that.'

Astrid examined the printed name on the card. 'Hamelin?'

'Their origins are from one of those former Soviet states that have infiltrated Western Europe since the end of the

Cold War. They started by contacting young women through social media networks, offering employment as receptionists, nannies or cleaners in England. But when they got to the UK, these women were forced to work in brothels. Now, this Hamelin gang has diversified their net to collect even more unfortunate people: economic migrants, refugees, vulnerable children and teenagers – sex traffickers are preying on a wider range of victims than ever before. Including runaways, of which there are many in the UK.'

Astrid returned the card to Ophelia. 'Do you have any individual names in this group?'

'Not yet, but I have an address in Harrow for part of their organisation. Do you want to check it with me?'

Astrid stared at Ophelia, her mind going over everything she'd heard while remembering the words she had in her jacket from the young woman called Zoe.

And her fear of what had happened to Olivia threatened to consume her.

18   ASTRID TAKES A TRAIN

They took the Tube, and then the train from Euston to Harrow. It was late, and the drunks were already rowdy in the carriage where Astrid and Ophelia sat.

Astrid ignored her reflection in the window and quizzed her new companion.

'What did the Agency hire you for?'

Ophelia shook her head. 'Is that a trick question? You know I can't tell you anything.'

'But you have worked for them?'

A drunk staggered past them, leering as he went.

'I can neither deny nor confirm that, Ms Snow, but if getting to know me will make you feel better about us working together, I'll allow you to ask me something personal.'

'You're not from London,' Astrid said. 'I can tell from your accent. Somewhere in the northeast?'

Ophelia laughed. 'You're cute when you go fishing.' Their legs touched as they sat opposite each other. 'I'm from a small village, one I was keen to get away from as quickly as possible.'

'Too parochial?'

'You could say that. There was an illness there, but it wasn't one of chemistry or biology unless you believe bigotry is inherent inside human DNA. It was accompanied by a secondary disease, that of silence. These twin ailments didn't affect everyone, but they affected enough. Eventually, I viewed its inhabitants as the living dead, walking emotional corpses to avoid. They shuffled around and glared at anyone who wasn't like them. I made myself invisible, and then I left.'

Before she could reply, Astrid heard the drunks in the next carriage singing racist football songs.

'I'm not sure there's anywhere where you can get away from those things.'

'You can if you look hard enough.' Ophelia tapped the side of her head. 'It's what's in here you can't escape from. I think you know that as well as anyone.' She placed her hand on the window and Astrid watched the damp drip down her skin. 'I was twelve years old when I realised something was different with me; sitting cross-legged and ankle-deep in the blood which wasn't mine, reciting the alphabet backwards. I could hear the siren song of the cattle reverberating around me, a lost lament for the world that could never be.

'From that day forward, everything appeared a lot paler to me, as if the very fabric of life had lost its sheen. Nature was dull and grey. The things a child should be interested in – toys and television and games and playing with others – were all utilitarian. The fact a twelve-year-old knew the meaning of utilitarianism tells you everything you need to know.

'Everywhere around me, people were trying to shine brighter than everybody else, to be significant in a world of insignificance. Yet, all I could see was the ever-increasing darkness drawing me closer to its cold gravitational pull. A black hole wasn't just a region in space where the force of gravity is so strong, light cannot escape; it was also deep inside me.'

Astrid gazed at this fascinating woman, still unsure if she was weaving a cleverly constructed tale of fiction for her benefit or telling the truth.

'Whose blood was it?'

'It was my father's. He'd slit his throat in front of me. I think it was to get back at my mother, and for one second, when he walked into the kitchen with that knife, I was sure he was going to kill me as well. But, ultimately, even he couldn't murder his only child. So I tried to save him, of course. That's why I was knee-deep in his blood when the police arrived. Reciting the alphabet backwards was my way of trying to control the situation, do you see?'

Astrid nodded. 'When I was in the family home, I started creating escape maps inside my mind – of all the ways I could get away from them. Sometimes they were fantasies I created as escapism, but others were avenues for me to make a new life for myself.'

'Did you create any maps where you killed him – Lawrence?'

'Of course. And they're still in my head.'

'Why don't you two lovely ladies come and join us in the next carriage?'

The drunk was unsteady on his feet, but he didn't slur his words.

Ophelia smiled at him. 'Bugger off, little man, before I embarrass you in front of all your mates.'

His face was frozen as he stood there, looking like the monster before Dr Frankenstein put the brain in. Then he stumbled off, swearing under his breath.

'Do you remember the first person you killed?' Ophelia said.

Astrid laughed. 'What makes you think I've killed anyone?'

Ophelia shook her head. 'I can see it in your eyes. And I might have read your Agency file.'

'Now I know you're lying. My Agency file was destroyed before I left them.'

As soon as the words came out of her mouth, Astrid knew it was a mistake.

She tricked me into revealing that.

'Do you want to hear about my first kill?'

Is this all a game to her, this mysterious Ophelia Red? Or is she manipulating me?

Astrid checked the time on her phone. 'Sure, why not? We've got another fifteen minutes on this train.'

Ophelia grinned at her. 'It was all because I saw the most beautiful woman in a bar. She was wearing a black-and-white striped top that was short-sleeved, so you could see the tattoos on her arms, and low enough for her pert bosom to be peaking out like low hanging fruit at the harvest. Figure-hugging trousers clung to her waist and legs, just begging to be removed slowly. She had curly blonde hair stolen from Monroe and crossed with Veronica Lake. Every set of eyes in the place was glued to her, including mine. There was a half-full cocktail glass in front of her on the table. She dropped her head towards it, wrapped her vibrant purple lips around the tip of the straw, and languidly sucked the rest of the remaining liquid deep into her throat.

'It was an intoxicating vision to behold, but she wasn't the reason I was there. She turned away for a second, which was all the time he needed, slipping something into the new drink he'd bought for her. She smiled and he grinned while I caressed the silver blade inside my jacket. His date finished her drink while he beamed at her and hooked one arm around her wrist. He dragged her from the seat as I saw her eyes glaze over. Then he winked at his two friends in the corner.'

Astrid peered into her face, remembering her encounter in the Korova nightclub while still tasting the drugs Jagger had put into her drink.

Ophelia Red continued. 'She was giddy, full of effervescent life and insouciance. She fell into his grasp while his accomplices slipped outside. He held her while she wrapped her languid arms around his neck. I followed them into the night. The others didn't hesitate to join him. I was right behind, but I was invisible to their eyes. The alley was on the immediate left of the bar. Strewn with empty beer bottles, disused needles and abandoned takeaway food. It was dark enough for them to be half-hidden in the gloom, but their perverted laughter gave them away. The shadows also helped me as I stepped forward and pushed the knife into the neck of the one closest to me. He dropped to the ground as the blood gushed out of him.

'I had the blade out of his flesh quicker than his partner could react, this time finding the soft part of his guts, tender as sliced lamb on the dinner plate. It cut through him with ease. His screams alerted the last bloke. He held his drugged victim as he turned to face me. I didn't let him speak, swiping the knife across his throat, and then catching the woman as he let go of her. The three of them wallowed in dirt as I took her out of that alley to the nearest hospital. Once I knew she was okay, I went home, ordered a curry, and sat watching old movies in front of the TV.'

Astrid considered Ophelia's words, peering into her deep blue eyes.

'You didn't have to kill them,' she said.

Ophelia grinned at her. 'Of course I did. What do you think would have happened if I'd let them go?'

Astrid shrugged. 'I don't know.'

'Yes, you do. They'd have done the same thing to other women. You know this.'

'So you're a vigilante?'

Ophelia lifted her bruised fingers to the window and ran them over the condensation.

'I'm many things, Astrid Snow – just like you.'

Astrid gazed at her, still unsure if anything she'd heard was truth or fiction.

'You said you were in that bar to save the woman from those men, but I think you were already there for them, regardless of her.'

Ophelia smiled. 'You're good at spotting the minor discrepancies in people's stories. Did the Agency teach you that?'

'I grew up in a household constructed of lies. Only the very best can hide the truth from me. So why don't you tell me the whole story?'

The train jerked forward, unsettling Astrid so she put her hand on Ophelia's leg. She removed it and settled back into her seat.

Ophelia's eyes sparkled like an azure sea.

'They'd assaulted other women, including a friend of mine, getting away with all of their crimes because their victims never went to the police, convinced they wouldn't be believed. So I handed out natural justice. Does that repulse you?'

Before Astrid could reply, the drunk returned with two of his mates.

'You tarts should snog each other right now so we can watch,' he said. His friends laughed in between drinking from cans of booze.

Ophelia stamped on his foot. Then she swung a hand up and caught the closest beer can to her, so it smashed into the bloke's jaw. The third one she left alone, his face frozen in shock as his mates howled in pain.

'It's probably best if you lads disappear now,' Astrid said.

They did without another word, and she knew they wouldn't be returning.

'Who are we going to see in Harrow?' Astrid said.

'A young lad I know,' Ophelia said. 'He's a member of a street gang – low-level drug dealing, but he knows something of these Hamelin people. He'll be able to point us in the right direction where some of these unfortunate women and girls are being held.'

'You could just give that address to the police?'

Ophelia narrowed her eyes. 'That won't achieve anything. The traffickers would only find new victims and put them in different premises. But, at least this way, we'll get the women away and into the hands of organisations that can help them, while discovering something useful about who we're searching for.'

The train rattled towards the station.

'You know this will get nasty, don't you?'

Ophelia's face lit up, and Astrid knew the redhead was looking forward to confrontation.

'You can't go easy on these people. We'll get the information we need by any means necessary. I was expecting to do this all on my own, but having you with me now will make it so much easier.'

'Do you have a weapon?' Astrid said.

Ophelia patted her jacket. 'Never go out unarmed. What about you?'

Astrid shook her head. 'I didn't think I'd be getting into a gang fight tonight.' She glanced out of the window as the train pulled into the station. 'What if we don't find what we're after?'

They got out of their seats together, their legs brushing once again. Ophelia grinned at her.

'Well, at least we'll have done some good by ridding the streets of these traffickers.'

Astrid grabbed her arm. 'I didn't come here to kill anyone.'

'Don't worry,' Ophelia said. 'You can leave that to me.'

As they stepped off the train into the London night, that's precisely what Astrid was worrying about.

19 ASTRID FORMS A PLAN

Astrid strode by Ophelia's side, watching as the dregs searched for somewhere else to drink in the early hours of Sunday morning.

'Where are we going?' she said.

Ophelia kicked an empty wine bottle out of their way.

'My contact lives nearby. He'll tell us where to find the brothel Hamelin has set up with their trafficking victims.'

The chill of the night nipped at Astrid's flesh. It was the type of coldness that reached into her bones to remind her just how far away she was from finding her niece and sister.

'Your contact from the National Crime Agency lives around here?'

Ophelia stopped outside a kebab shop, the smell of the grilled meat drifting out and settling over Astrid.

'I can't wait to see young Baz's face when I tell him you thought he worked for the NCA.'

Astrid shook her head. 'Okay, so you've got some kid, probably a drug dealer, working for you. That still doesn't explain why somebody at the NCA is feeding you this information about Hamelin instead of dealing with the organisation themselves.'

'It's not rocket science. I can handle these criminals in a way the police or the NCA can't. You know what it's like.'

An aroma of garlic and chilli seeped out of the shop behind them.

'Is that what it's like for you: vigilante justice as long as you get paid for it?'

Ophelia pressed her finger into Astrid's shoulder.

'I'm not getting paid to find Kate and, to make sure there's no confusion between us before we begin, I'll do anything to find her. Just like you will to find your niece and sister.' She removed her hand from Astrid. 'Or perhaps you're not too bothered about your sister.'

Astrid didn't argue with her. 'How far away is this Baz?'

Ophelia grinned. 'We're here.' She strode into the kebab shop, past the customers and staff, into a back room and up the stairs. There was a door at the top, which she knocked on. 'Do you want to eat?'

Astrid said no as the door opened and a kid of about fourteen stared at them. Somebody had taken garden shears to his dark hair, while spots of blood circled the space between his eyes and his cheeks.

'You could have brought me some chips, Oppie.'

'Next time, Baz,' Ophelia said as she pushed past him and into the room.

Astrid followed her as he closed the door. She peered at the stains on the wall and the unmade bed, turning her nose up at the rotten smell coming from the bathroom. Then she saw the packets of pills on the table, all different colours and placed inside their containers. She looked at the boy.

'Where are your parents?'

As soon as she said it, she thought about what her reply

would have been if some stranger had asked her the same question at that age.

But I wasn't dealing drugs.

Yet I was a criminal.

Baz shrugged. 'They left.' He grinned at her through crooked teeth. 'But they taught me a valuable lesson before they buggered off.'

'What's that?' Astrid said.

He went to the table and picked up a bag of purple pills.

'Always be ambitious.' She couldn't argue with that. 'Everybody I know wants to be a gangster. Everyone's seen it on TV, and that's what they want to be. They look at music videos, and it looks like the people in them are making hundreds of thousands of pounds, although the reality is they're still living at their mum's house. Most come from estates and they see their parents working in dead-end jobs, struggling to pay the bills. They get home, their mum's not there, and all the places where kids could play are closing down. Nine times out of ten, they leave school without qualifications. So if you're broke, if you can't get a job, you're going to take the opportunity. That's all I'm doing. And I only sell to adults; not to kids, but to those who know what they're doing. It's their choice. I'm not like these blokes you're after.'

'Hamelin?' Astrid said.

The kid nodded. 'The Pied Piper, you know?' He lifted his hands to his mouth and played with an invisible pipe. 'They're recruiting kids to do their dirty work for them; one's even younger than me. The way it works is the elders take you under their wing, getting children acting as look-outs or tricking other kids and women into the group with promises of cash, drugs or jobs. Then they're forced into slavery or selling sex. The young kids become part of it, looking at those older than them and admiring the adults, getting the rewards for being part of the enterprise, but feeling proud about it as well. They get respect from their peers, which is just as important as money. They look up to the adults, thinking *that could be me in a few years. I could get a promotion – loyalty brings royalty.*'

As Astrid listened to him, she saw the pain filling his eyes, noticed the trembling in his cheeks and how his lips quivered as he spoke.

'This has happened to some of your friends?'

Baz wiped at his mouth. 'Yeah. And it could have been me if I hadn't found something else.' He glanced at the piles of pills. 'So what are you two going to do about them?'

Ophelia smiled and slapped him on the back.

'Don't worry, mate. Me and Snowstorm will sort them out.'

Astrid glared at her as Baz spoke.

'Snowstorm?'

'A nickname I got when I was your age,' Astrid said.

'See,' Ophelia said, 'we'll blow these Hamelin scumbags out of this city.' Her hand was still on his shoulder. 'All we need is for you to give us the address of one of their brothels, and then we'll do the rest. After that, you won't have to worry about anything.'

He glanced between the two women, and Astrid guessed he was wondering if this would make things better or worse for him and his community.

'You won't mention this came from me?'

'Of course not, Baz. You know you can always trust me. You're like the little brother I never had.'

She put her arms around him and hugged. Astrid watched them, unsure who looked the more uncomfortable before Ophelia let go. Then he leant into Ophelia and whispered to her. She came away with a smile and nodded at Astrid. Then she left Baz behind, leaving the flat and the kebab shop.

'Is it far?' Astrid said when they got outside.

'Five minutes from here,' Ophelia said. 'A converted two-storey former house, now with dozens of individual rooms supposedly used for the homeless and the unemployed.'

'And the police don't know about this?' Astrid said.

'Not yet. Hamelin's informers in the police let them know when a raid is coming, so they move before it arrives. That's why they're always a step ahead of the authorities.' She grinned at Astrid. 'But not us tonight.'

She set off and Astrid marched by her side.

'Have you got a plan?'

Ophelia shook her head. 'I thought once we get a look at the building, you might whip up one of those escape maps of yours.'

Astrid grabbed her arm and pushed her into the front of an abandoned shop. The metal frame rattled and sent rats scuttling out of the shadows.

'Who told you I used to be called Snowstorm?'

She didn't wriggle out of Astrid's grip.

'I told you, I've read your Agency file.'

'And I said that was destroyed.'

'Apparently, someone kept copies,' Ophelia said.

Astrid let go of her, struggling to control her breathing.

'We need to have a long talk once this is over.'

Ophelia rubbed her hands together.

'Oh, good. Will it be over a bottle of wine and a candlelit dinner? I'll have steak, rare, so the blood seeps out of it with one flick of my knife.'

Astrid ignored the question. 'Show me where this brothel is.'

They crossed the road, Ophelia leading her down an alley, through a rubbish-strewn passage stinking of unemptied bins, and into an unlit street. As Ophelia pointed to their destination, half a dozen parked cars were before them.

'It's the one on the end. All the rest are empty.'

Astrid stared at it, watching as a car parked outside. Two men got out and entered the building.

'Customers or gang members?' Astrid said.

Ophelia stepped out of the shadows. 'We'll soon find out.'

Astrid pulled her back. 'Wait. We need a plan.'

'Don't you have one?'

Astrid resisted the temptation to punch her in the face.

'I know nothing about the layout of the place or who's inside.'

'It doesn't matter. We go in, crack a few heads and get the information we want. But, of course, whoever's in charge of Hamelin won't be in there. It will be just low-level thugs and functionaries, but they should be able to tell us something useful about who runs this operation.'

Astrid glared at her. 'Is this how you always work?'

Ophelia shrugged. 'I've been doing this for fifteen years, and it's always turned out fine.'

'How old are you?'

'Twenty-eight.'

'You started when you were thirteen?'

Ophelia nodded. 'Once the old man was out of the way, I had to have a hobby. What else was a girl to do?'

'Okay. We need to check the front and back of the building before going inside. Focus on the windows and the doors to see if any bodies are visible. Also, check the buildings on either side to ensure there aren't any lookouts stationed there.'

'You want us to split up?'

'It will be quicker for now. Then we can meet back here and come up with a plan. Okay?'

Ophelia raised a hand to the side of her face and gave Astrid a mock salute. Then she turned away and dashed across the road, using the shadows as protection. Astrid watched her go, still wondering what she'd let herself in for. Then she pictured the last time she'd seen Olivia and her heart sank into the pit of her stomach again.

She made her way down the street, walking as if she was heading home after a night out, glancing at the brothel. Then, when she was opposite and saw nobody outside or in the windows, she moved towards the car that been had parked near the building a few minutes ago.

Astrid pushed up against the vehicle, peering inside and realising the door was unlocked.

For a quick getaway.

Then she looked into the flickering lights of the house.

What's the likely number of security they'd have in there to guard the women? Four? Six? Eight?

Even with Ophelia to help her, six to eight thugs would be too many for them to handle without weapons.

And she didn't trust Ophelia, unsure if she was unhinged or not.

She was quick to tell me about the people she'd killed in that alley.

If what she said was true.

Astrid was peering at the building when she heard the screams erupt from inside. Women were shouting, followed by men speaking in a foreign language.

Then the gunshots came.

And more screaming and shouting.

Astrid sprinted across the street, ran up the steps and barged through the front door. She hit a wall as she fell inside, her shoulder cracking off it and sending a surge of electricity through her body. She was standing in an empty hallway, with all the noise coming from upstairs.

She staggered to the stairs, her hand on the rail when she glanced up at the man above her.

The man who pointed a gun at her.

20 ASTRID CREATES A STORM

The man garbled an insult at her. She didn't understand the language, but she got the meaning. Mania possessed his eyes and his hand trembled, giving Astrid the split second she needed to move her head as he fired the gun. The bullet sped past her face, scorching her ear as she pressed her shoulder into the bannister. Then she thrust her palm up and knocked the weapon from him. It tumbled to the side as he fell on her, taking them off the stairs and into the filth-strewn carpet.

Astrid's head vibrated as she rolled across the floor, scrambling for the gun before he got it. Her vision was blurred as the shouting and screaming continued upstairs. She scrambled up, searching for her attacker, but unable to locate him.

Then something hard hit her in the back, the force of it throwing her forward and down the stairs. His hands were on her throat, his sweaty face pushed into her hair.

'Stupid bitch,' he said in a guttural accent.

She dug her fingers into the carpet as he sank his teeth into her neck. He bit down as she threw all of her weight back. It was enough for them to stagger into the wall as Astrid twisted her elbow into his gut and hurled him off her. Blood seeped out of the injury as a fire ripped through her flesh. She spun around to see him grinning at her, his face blood-red, his eyes glaring yellow. He opened his mouth, about to speak when she lunged forward and stamped on his jaw. The bone crunched as teeth and blood flew, Astrid striking again, kicking hard into his cheek.

He collapsed into a heap.

'Fuck!' She rubbed at the wound, staring at the blood on her fingers.

Her head throbbed as she struggled to breathe, listening to the silence. She didn't wait around, running upstairs two at a time, her eyes darting everywhere, searching for danger, finding terrified female faces peering at her from open doorways. Astrid moved forward, nearly falling over the bodies: two men with blood and brains leaking from their crushed skulls.

Should I go back down to get that gun?

A gunshot from the end of the passage dragged her attention that way. The screams that followed were both male and female. She was going to move when a bloke staggered towards her. His eyes were wild, a pistol in his trembling fingers. His free hand found the wall for stability, dragging blood across it as he realised she was in front of him. He mumbled something in that same foreign language, glaring at Astrid as he pointed the gun at her. She waited for the bullet, digging her nails into her palms, knowing she'd let Olivia down again. She didn't think about her sister. All she could see in her head was Olivia's smile. The blood dripped from her hands as the man stumbled closer, finger on the trigger and glee in his eyes.

Then he fell at her feet, his face smacking into the

carpet.

Astrid saw the knife sticking out of his back.

Ophelia stepped forward, reached down and removed the blade from the body, wiping it on his clothes.

'I've had this since I was twelve.' She winked at Astrid. 'It's a family heirloom.'

Astrid steadied herself against the wall. 'Are there any more guards?'

Ophelia shrugged as if she'd been asked what flavour cookie she liked.

'I don't know. I didn't check downstairs. Weren't you doing that?'

'How did you get up here?'

'There's a ladder out the back. I thought it would give me the element of surprise.'

If Astrid's body hadn't been so weak, she'd have pushed Ophelia Red down those stairs to see what was there.

'Make sure nobody comes up while I check here,' Astrid said.

Without waiting for a reply, she turned away, heading for the first room. The door was open, the room barely lit, but she saw the young woman trembling on the bed. There was nobody else there.

'Are you okay?' Astrid said. The woman nodded. 'What's your name?'

'Jenny,' she said through shivering lips.

Astrid sat next to her. 'You're safe now, Jenny. I'm going to get you out of here.'

'What about the men?' Jenny said.

'How many are there?' Astrid said.

Jenny shrugged. 'I'm not sure. They don't let me out of this room. At least six of them.'

Which means there has to be more downstairs. Probably

with guns.

Astrid got up. 'I'll close the door behind me, Jenny. Don't open it until I come back.'

If I come back.

'Okay,' Jenny said.

Astrid closed the door, checking the other rooms on that floor as Ophelia guarded the stairs. She discovered more scared women and girls, but no men, talking to all of them, trying her best to make them feel safe. She wasn't sure if it worked. Then she returned to Ophelia.

'Anything downstairs?'

'Male voices,' Ophelia said. 'Speaking Romanian.'

'Do you understand what they're saying?'

She nodded. 'A little. I think there are four of them, but they don't have guns. They were for the security up here that we took care of.'

'I left one downstairs,' Astrid said.

Ophelia pointed at the floor. 'No matter. We have one here, and there's another further down the passage.'

Astrid glanced at the body near her feet. 'How many did you kill?'

'Three. You?'

'One.'

Ophelia moved from the stairs and reached down for the gun before offering it to Astrid. Astrid had never liked guns, but had used them when she had to – so she took it.

'We can't go down,' Ophelia said. 'We'll be sitting ducks. Unless they leave.'

'No,' Astrid said. 'They won't do that with their merchandise here. They'll come for us soon, but we can't hang around. It won't be long before someone tells the police about the gunfire.'

'I'll go back down the ladder. Create a distraction for

you to charge down the stairs and get them from this end,' Ophelia said.

'What if they're waiting for you?'

Ophelia pulled at her hair as if she was about to go on a first date. Then she waved the gun in front of her.

'Bang, bang, they're dead.'

I'd wanted to do this without excessive violence, but that was naïve. And there are still victims below.

Astrid cradled the pistol in her hand. 'Okay.'

Ophelia beamed at her. 'Be a snowstorm.'

Then she was off down the passage, dodging corpses and climbing out of the window. Astrid moved to the top of the stairs, pushing into the wall and waiting.

She didn't have to wait long.

Gunfire echoed around the building, mixed in with the angry shouting of male Romanian voices. Astrid bounced down the stairs, rebounding off the wall as she hit the bottom, swivelling her body and arm a complete three hundred and sixty degrees. The gun travelled the distance with her, searching out the enemy, but finding the hall empty.

Astrid turned and ran towards the gunshots, seeing men ahead of her firing at Ophelia, who was crouching behind a large fridge-freezer. She raised her hand and brought the pistol down across the neck of the nearest man. Pain jumped through her wrist when she connected with him: it hurt, but it must have been worse for him as he buckled.

The bloke to her left snapped his head towards her as Astrid smashed the gun into his nose. Blood and bone burst everywhere as she continued forward and pushed him into the third shooter. The two of them hit the wall and then the ground. Astrid kicked the weapons out of their hands while checking there weren't any others.

Ophelia came out from behind the fridge-freezer.

'You watch them while I look through the rooms on this floor.'

Astrid watched her go before focusing on the two men whining at her feet. The other one was out cold.

Ophelia returned two minutes later. 'Just scared women and girls – no blokes.' She spoke to the only one who was unharmed. 'Who do you work for?'

He replied in broken English. 'Don't know. All contact through texts.'

'Texts?' Astrid said.

He reached for his jacket, stopping as Ophelia waved her gun at him.

'No funny stuff.'

The man removed a mobile and handed it to Astrid.

'Texts on there. And payments. No other contact.'

'Where did you get the phone from?' Astrid said.

He lowered his face before Ophelia kicked him in the side.

'Who gave you the mobile?'

His lips trembled as he spoke. 'Kabak. They control everything and everyone.'

'Aren't you worried they'll punish you for telling us this?' Astrid said.

She peered into his eyes and understood his fear wasn't of her and Ophelia.

'No. The Kabak don't care if you know who they are. They'll kill you for this.'

'The Kabak are a family?' Astrid said.

He nodded. 'Old Romanian family.'

Ophelia placed her foot on his leg. 'Where are they based?'

He pointed at the phone. 'All on there.'

Astrid flicked across the screen and it came to life, asking for a security fingerprint. She held it out to the bloke, who obliged, and she stared at the only app icon on the device: the letters KC.

'What's that?' Ophelia said.

'KabakChat,' he said.

'A custom-made secret criminal communication system,' Astrid said. 'I've seen this type of thing before. Users have access to self-destructing texts that delete after a certain length of time. There's also a panic wipe, where all the data is deleted by entering a four-digit code.'

She opened the app, scrolling through the messages, but they were all in Romanian. She handed it to Ophelia.

'Can you read any of them?'

'Sure. They're all pretty short, but the last few are the interesting ones.' She showed the screen to Astrid, who only shrugged. 'There's a shipment coming into the city tonight in an hour. One of these goons is supposed to go to the rendezvous point to meet somebody from the Kabak family.'

Astrid turned from her and went to the bloke whose nose she'd broken.

'Phone,' she said to him.

He didn't argue, reaching into his pocket and giving it to her. Then she moved to the unconscious one and removed his mobile.

'You're going to leave them alive?' Ophelia said.

'I'm not a murderer.'

Ophelia shook her head. 'What about their victims?'

'I'll get them all down here, and then call the police on one of these phones. You can lock these three in a room with no window. Okay?'

She narrowed her eyes and peered at Astrid for thirty seconds.

Then she grinned. 'I can do that, partner.'

Astrid left her to it and went to free the women and girls. She had to work hard to convince them they were safe; their faces contorted with terror when they saw the bodies of their jailers.

She got everyone into the large room at the front of the house. Then she called the police and left an anonymous tip before leaving the same message with the BBC and the local news.

When she finished, Ophelia joined her at the door.

'Are they all okay?'

'As well as they can be,' Astrid said. 'What about you?'

'I feel great,' Ophelia said. 'Though I'd be better if we'd left none of them alive.'

Astrid peered at her. 'They might not know a lot, but the police may get something from them and one of these phones.' She placed all but one mobile on a table at the front door, ensuring it wasn't security locked before putting the other in her pocket. 'Do you know where the rendezvous point is?'

'Thirty minutes' drive from here at an industrial park. But we don't have a car.'

Astrid smiled. 'That's not a problem.'

She stepped outside, went to the car closest to the house, and opened the unlocked door.

'Keys?' Ophelia said.

Astrid removed a set from her pocket. 'They were next to one of those secret phones.'

She took a deep breath and thought of the people they'd just rescued, feeling nothing for those they'd killed.

Now she had a rendezvous with the Kabak and, hopefully, information on where her niece was.

21 ASTRID GETS A PHONE NUMBER

Astrid drove as Ophelia talked.

'I shouldn't have left those three scumbags alive.'

'Are you a psychopath?' Astrid said.

Ophelia laughed. 'With all your training, can't you tell?'

Astrid stared at her in the rear-view mirror. 'It's hard to say with you.'

'I said I shouldn't have left them alive not because I wanted to kill them – though that was tempting – but because when the police turn up, they'll give them our descriptions. And that might cause trouble later on.'

'They won't say anything. They think we'll be dead soon enough, anyway. So we don't matter to them anymore. Plus, it's embarrassing for them, being taken down by two women.'

'What about the victims? They'll tell the police about us.'

Astrid shook her head. 'I doubt they can remember too much, especially about you.' She stopped the car at a red light. 'We have nothing to worry about there.'

'Okay,' Ophelia said. She reached across and turned the radio on, fiddling through the stations.

'Leave it there,' Astrid said when she heard Bowie singing about life on Mars.

'Isn't this a bit before your time?'

Astrid laughed. 'The classics are good for all ages.'

Ophelia glanced at herself in the mirror, pulling at her hair to straighten out a wayward curl.

'I always preferred Iggy Pop to Bowie. Not the Stooges stuff, but his solo career.'

The light changed to green. 'Iggy wouldn't have had a solo career without Bowie.'

'True,' Ophelia said. 'But Iggy had that sense of danger, that frisson in him that made you think everything could go wrong at any second and the world would end around you, that the former Mr Jones never had.' Her eyes sparkled as she spoke. 'I've watched the video of *Lust for Life* live in Manchester in 1977 more times than I can remember. One of his crew carries him slumped to the mic, holds him there for a minute before Iggy opens up after twelve bars of intro and hypnotises the audience as if it's an out-of-body experience that will engulf them all. It's mesmerising.' She pushed her leg closer to Astrid's. 'I guess I'm your passenger now.'

Astrid laughed again. 'And it's gone past midnight, sister.'

Ophelia laughed with her. There was a warmth between them Astrid hadn't felt with anybody else for a while.

But still at the back of her mind was the question of Olivia and Courtney. If they'd been drawn into the dangerous world of people trafficking because of Courtney's friendship with Vanessa Moore, Astrid didn't want to think too hard about what had happened to them. All she focused on as she drove was helping as many victims of this Hamelin organisation – the Kabak family – as she could.

The music changed and James Brown tried to convince anybody listening to him how much of a man's world it was.

'Have you thought what you'll do if we don't get information from these Kabak people about Kate or your missing family?' Ophelia said.

Astrid had thought of little else.

'Vanessa Moore was getting trafficking victims away from their captors, and this Hamelin group is the biggest trafficker in the city – they must know something about her. If we can find her, I'm hoping we'll find Olivia.'

'Not your sister?'

'And Courtney.' She turned towards Ophelia. 'But if you think Kate Gregory went to Paul Jagger, why do you believe Hamelin will know anything about her?'

'It's a hunch, and I always trust my hunches. Just like I did with you.'

'Me?'

'Sure. My gut told me I could trust you, and look how that has worked out for us.'

So far.

Their destination was five minutes away.

'You didn't follow the plan at the house,' Astrid said.

'If an opportunity arises, act on instinct.'

'Is that what Iggy taught you?'

The music changed to Chic singing about *Good Times*, and Ophelia Red moved her head from side to side to the rhythm.

'Girls will be girls, Astrid, and unlike you, I never had a secret government organisation to teach me how to navigate through the murky depths of the underworld.'

'So who taught you?'

'Why, Ms Snow, I'll have you know I'm a self-taught woman. That and watching thousands of hours of Bruce Lee and James Bond movies has got me to where I am today.'

'What's your job title?'

'The same as yours, I guess – a freelance problem solver.'

'How did you end up working for the Agency?'

'Guess,' Ophelia said.

'You did some black ops work for a recognised counter-intelligence organisation and the Agency got your contact details from them?'

Ophelia lifted her hands, moving her fingers around as if playing an invisible keyboard.

'I can neither confirm nor deny your accusation, Ms Snow. Next question.'

Astrid glanced through the windscreen at the run-down industrial park ahead of them. It seemed empty of people and vehicles, so she parked a few hundred yards from the entrance, hidden in the shadows.

'You haven't told me how you became a professional killer.'

'Are we still in that process of getting to know each other, Astrid? Or is this because I read your Agency file and know all about you while you know nothing about me?'

'I know your father killed himself in front of you when you were twelve. I know how you made your first kills to save a woman who'd had her glass spiked in a bar.'

Ophelia moved her head up and down like a nodding dog as Prince sang about purple rain.

'That's only if what I told you was true.'

Astrid was about to reply when she saw a car drive into the industrial estate. She turned the music off as a large truck drove in behind it. A driver stepped out, a small bald man who went to the gap between the car and the back of the truck.

'Let's get closer,' Astrid said.

They got out of the car, moving through the shadows, sticking close to the bushes and trees. She touched Ophelia's arm and they stopped a hundred yards from the vehicles. Two men stepped out of the car, so similar in appearance, Astrid guessed they must be brothers. The taller was over six feet, slicked-back dark hair, with the chiselled features of a movie star. The smaller one had an unkempt beard with a toilet-brush hairstyle. Astrid estimated they were in their early thirties.

Ophelia whispered in her ear. 'Kabak?'

Astrid didn't reply, still watching as the men spoke to the driver before he went to open the back of the truck, which was forty feet long and ten feet wide. She heard the squeak of the metal as he unlocked the container. Before he opened the doors, a woman got out of the front of the car. She was small, just over five feet, with grey hair and so many marks on her face, Astrid could see the dark lines from where she was. She clutched a clipboard full of papers and waved a pen around.

Then all four of them spoke in Romanian.

Astrid kept her voice low. 'Can you understand them?'

Ophelia nodded. 'They're going to check the merchandise. That's why she has those papers in her hand.'

Phantom fingers grasped Astrid's heart at the thought of Olivia being inside somewhere like that truck. She glanced away from the traffickers towards the barrier surrounding the industrial estate.

'There's a gap in the fence opposite the truck. So you go

through that and approach them from one side while I take the front,' Astrid said.

'And then?' Ophelia said.

Astrid removed the gun from her jacket. 'And then we get the truth.'

They went their separate ways, Astrid hesitating a second to make sure Ophelia got to the fence and through it unnoticed. Then Ophelia crept up to the truck as Astrid stepped from the shadows and into the industrial estate. The driver opened the doors, with the four of them too engrossed to notice her approaching.

Astrid looked beyond them, peering into the darkness in the container, her heart tightening at what she saw: more than a dozen shivering, trembling bodies, their eyes blinking in the gloom as they held each other. She gripped the gun as the woman wrote something on the paper on her clipboard.

'I thought you'd have gone paperless for your inventory,' Astrid said as she pointed the weapon at them.

The four of them looked at her. Fear consumed the driver's face while the others were unmoved. Then the one with the movie-star looks spoke.

'Who are you?'

She waved the gun at him. 'You first.'

Astrid watched as the men turned to the grey-haired woman, looking for guidance. Ophelia lingered behind them in the shadows of the truck.

The woman attached her pen to the clipboard. 'How did you know we'd be here?'

Astrid steadied the pistol while removing the phone from her pocket.

'I shut down one of your brothels and took this from the men before I killed them.'

The men's faces went white, but the woman was unflinching.

'Do you know who we are?' she said.

Astrid returned the mobile to her jacket. 'You're the Kabak, also known as Hamelin.'

The woman grinned as if Astrid was Red Riding Hood and she was the wolf about to eat her.

'I'm Elena Kabak, and these are my sons, Andrei and Mihai.' She went to them, running a hand over their cheeks. 'Don't you think Mihai is so handsome he could be a movie star?'

She never looked at the driver. Behind them, sobbing came from the back of the truck.

'I'm sure he'll be popular where he's going,' Astrid said.

Elena Kabak gazed into her. 'And where is that?'

Astrid stepped closer to them. 'You're all off to prison, but not before you tell me something.'

She nodded to Ophelia, who moved out of the shadows, her gun pointed straight at Elena Kabak's head. The brothers swore together, but their mother didn't flinch.

'Are you sisters?' Elena said.

Ophelia pushed her phone towards them, a photo of Kate Gregory on the screen.

'Do you know this girl?'

'Why would we?' Mihai said.

Astrid saw Ophelia's finger tremble on the trigger.

'Because you scumbags traffic young women and girls, and she's missing.'

Mihai shrugged. 'They all look the same to me.'

Ophelia lifted the gun and brought it down on his nose. The bone cracked and blood seeped out of it as he fell into his brother. While they held each other, Astrid lowered her weapon and removed her phone. She found a recent picture of Olivia and Courtney together. She stuck it into Elena's pockmarked face.

'Do you recognise them?'

Elena shook her head. 'I only know names. That's why I keep the records.' She glanced at her sons as Mihai wiped the blood from his face. 'My boys tell me to be more modern, to go digital, but those things are too easy to trace. Paper and pen are all you need.' She removed the pen from the clipboard. 'Give me their names and I'll tell you if we've processed them.' She looked again at the photo. 'Though the girl is far too young for our merchandise.' She smiled at Astrid. 'We're not monsters.'

Astrid resisted the urge to do what Ophelia had and told Elena Kabak the names instead.

'Courtney and Olivia Snow, plus Kate Gregory.'

Elena went through her papers while her sons whispered to each other in Romanian. Astrid stood and waited, keeping one eye on the brothers while the other focused on Ophelia, hoping the redhead wouldn't lose control and do something stupid.

It was two minutes of searching that seemed like an eternity. Astrid's arm ached and her legs throbbed, while a loud echoing boom bounced around inside her head, buzzing through her brain like a thousand angry bees about to sting the back of her eyes.

Elena Kabak's voice broke the spell. 'They are not on my list.'

Ophelia scowled and seized the clipboard from her. 'Let me look.'

It was enough of a distraction for the brothers to act. Mihai threw himself at Ophelia while Andrei grabbed Astrid's arm. His fingers dug through her clothes and into her skin, gripping like a vice. Astrid dropped her gun as

Ophelia fell under Mihai's weight, the clipboard and pen clattering to the ground as they did.

Astrid pushed Andrei into the car, smashing his elbow into the glass before head-butting him. Her forehead cracked into his nose, drawing blood from both of them, but forcing him to let go of her. She jerked back, lifting her leg to kick him, but he grabbed her foot and twisted her around. He tossed her back and she stumbled into Elena Kabak, sending both of them into the dirt.

'*Mamă*,' he shouted.

As he bent his legs to help her, Astrid jumped up, swivelled her hips and kicked him in the side of the head. She heard his neck crack before her foot returned to the ground. He tumbled in a heap next to his mother. Astrid gave both of them one brief look before turning to Ophelia.

'You could have been a dancer,' Ophelia said as she stood over Mihai with a bloodied pen in her hand. There was a gaping hole where Mihai's left eye should have been. Ophelia glanced at her handiwork. 'There'll be no career in movies for him now, I guess. An extra in a horror movie, perhaps.'

Astrid stepped over him and went to the vehicle. The driver had disappeared. She climbed inside, using the torch on her phone to illuminate the darkness. The huddled mass of scared, shivering women and girls removed any guilt she might have felt for the dead Kabak brothers. She took out the phone from the brothel and texted the address to the police. Then she dropped it in the truck and helped everybody out.

'You're safe now,' she said to them all.

She saw Ophelia going through Elena Kabak's records when she stepped down.

'Any luck?' she said.

Ophelia's cheeks were as red as her hair. 'They're not here.' She threw the clipboard to the ground, still clutching the bloodied pen as she pulled Kabak away from her dead sons. 'Are you working with Paul Jagger?'

The old woman's face was tear-stained.

'Jagger? He doesn't deal with the likes of us. We're not British enough for him.'

Ophelia let her go, glancing at the women huddled together.

'Have you contacted the police?'

Astrid nodded. 'They'll be here soon. We should leave and start again tomorrow.'

'Start where?' Ophelia said.

'We'll think of something.' Astrid sounded more confident than she felt.

Ophelia pointed the bloodied pen at Elena Kabak. 'We should kill her.'

'No,' Astrid said. 'Let the police and the NCA question her. Then they can finally end her organisation.'

Elena Kabak craned her neck at Astrid. 'Someone else will only replace us.' She stared at the victims her family had brought into the country. 'You can't prevent this with your pitiful laws.' She glanced at her dead sons. 'People like you will never be as strong as us.'

Before Astrid could stop her, Ophelia had plunged the pen into Elena Kabak's leg. The woman screamed and collapsed as Ophelia pulled the pen from the wound.

'Fuck!' Astrid said.

But she didn't go to help Kabak as she lay screaming next to the bodies of her sons.

'It's okay,' Ophelia said. 'I didn't aim for an artery.' She grinned at Elena. 'She'll be fine once they pump the painkillers into her.' Then she went to Astrid. 'Do you have a piece of paper?'

Astrid took a deep breath to control her anger, hearing police sirens in the distance, but getting closer.

'Why?'

'I'll give you my phone number and we can meet up later today.'

Astrid glanced at the papers on the clipboard, knowing the police would need those for their evidence. She reached into her jacket, moving past Zoe's letter and finding the paper she'd discovered in Courtney's house. She handed it to Ophelia.

'What's this?' Ophelia said. 'VAN and GUARD?'

Astrid told her where she'd found it. 'I don't know what it means. Perhaps Courtney or Vanessa Moore hired somebody to protect the women and girls they rescued from the traffickers.'

Ophelia gazed at the text for thirty seconds. 'Unless it isn't two words, but one.'

'Vanguard?' Astrid said.

'It could be.' Ophelia used the bloody pen to write her mobile number on the paper and returned it to Astrid. 'We can talk about it later. Are you going to your hotel?'

Astrid nodded. She couldn't remember the last time she'd rested.

'What about you?'

Ophelia took Astrid's arm and pulled her away from Elena Kabak.

'I have to see Baz and tell him everything is okay. I'll sleep at his place and wait for your call.' She looked outside the fence. 'You take the car.'

'I can drop you off,' Astrid said.

Ophelia let go of her. 'I'm fine walking. I need the fresh air to clear my head.'

Astrid touched her hand. 'I'm glad we didn't find Kate, Olivia or Courtney here or on their list. It would have been too awful to bear.'

'But we still don't know where they are,' Ophelia said.

'We'll find them, I'm sure of it.'

She wasn't, but Astrid couldn't tell her that.

The police sirens grew closer as they strode through the entrance.

'Later,' Ophelia said as she broke away and headed into the shadows.

Astrid got into the car, started the engine and reached for the radio, listening to Polly Jean Harvey singing about the danger ahead.

Astrid left the car half a mile away from the hotel. She didn't go straight to her room, lingering outside an all-night petrol station instead. The neon lights flickered around her as she watched drivers filling up their cars while a few who'd been turfed out of the pubs went inside to find more refreshments.

She pushed her back into the wall, feeling the chill of the early morning – it had just turned three o'clock – and focusing on those in the petrol station. Astrid had never known stability or normality, had found little time to relax or enjoy herself before something dragged her into a world of pain and disappointment. So watching ordinary people doing normal things, even at this time of the day, intrigued her – especially after what she'd gone through not so long ago.

A young man and woman came out of the garage, holding hands and laughing as they got into a car, and Astrid wondered if she'd ever have a life like that; she questioned if she even wanted a life like that. Back at her hotel, she had a small backpack that contained all she owned in the world. She had money in several bank accounts, some of which, ironically, had come from her mother when she'd died, but most was what she'd taken with her on leaving the Agency. Yet, she never spent money on anything besides hotels and eating semi-regularly. And the occasional drink.

As she thought of that, her stomach rumbled, telling her to go into the garage and get something to take back to her hotel room.

But no booze.

She needed to keep a clear head for later.

Astrid went in and bought a large packet of prawn cocktail crisps and an out-of-date ham sandwich. Then, for good measure, she got a litre bottle of Coke in case she decided to stay awake for most of the morning.

She took them back to the hotel, switching on the TV when she got inside. She ate half of the sandwich as she flicked through channels to see if there was any news on what she and Ophelia had done. There was nothing about it and the same when she checked online using her phone.

Astrid glugged Coke from the bottle to take away the taste of the plastic ham while thinking about the mysterious Ophelia Red. She removed the paper from her pocket with Ophelia's phone number on it, staring at the bloodstains around the edge.

Then she peered at the words she'd given little thought to since discovering them in Courtney's house.

VAN and GUARD or VANGUARD?

She opened Google on her phone and typed VANGUARD into the search box. Two billion results came back.

Two billion.

The first page was filled with details about an investment advisor group of the same name.

Was Courtney investing in assets and hedge funds?

That seemed about as likely as her sister helping the victims of people trafficking.

But there was the money their mother had left them in her will. And what they'd shared from the sale of the house. Not that Astrid had seen Courtney during either event. She didn't go to her mother's funeral and hadn't visited the grave.

And I never will.

So perhaps Courtney had been using Vanguard as an investment opportunity.

The Coke slipped down her throat as Astrid tried another search, this time adding Courtney's name to Vanguard.

No results found for "vanguard + Courtney Snow."

She sighed, even though that wasn't unexpected. Then she tried a different search.

There were twenty-four thousand results for "Ophelia Red", none of which were useful – clothes, wine, a hurricane, and even an ultra-limited edition Germanium Fuzz Pedal.

Astrid dropped her phone on the bedside table and turned the TV off.

Ophelia Red.

Some of what she told me was true, some of it was lies.

But which was which? I'm good at spotting dishonesty but not with her.

She's a trained killer, that's obvious – so who trained her?

Astrid didn't believe that line Ophelia had said about being self-taught. And the damaged fingers must have been pain inflicted a long time ago.

She peered at the phone number again.

Perhaps it would be best to lose that.

She reached over and turned the light off, lying on the bed without getting undressed. A thousand unanswered questions bounced around inside her head, all of which kept her hyperactive brain awake for most of the night. Eventually, she slept, but it was an uncomfortable rest.

ASTRID WOKE AT EIGHT, crawled off the bed and removed her clothes. Then she spent twenty minutes under a hot shower, hoping the water would clean away the dirt of her recent encounters while sparking her mind into action. She was dressed and drying her hair when the knock came.

Who knows I'm here?

Ophelia?

She went to the door, opening it without hesitation, surprised to see Chief Inspector Thorn. At least she wasn't in uniform.

'Do you have news about Olivia and Courtney?'

'It's best if we talk inside.'

Astrid stepped aside. 'Be my guest, Jude.'

Thorn entered and Astrid closed the door. The Chief Inspector glanced around the room.

'Somebody took down a high-level trafficking gang in the early hours of the morning. Do you know anything about that?'

Astrid went to the window and opened the curtains. It was bright sunshine outside and the rays warmed her face.

'Is that why you're here, Jude?'

'Did you get what you wanted from Paul Jagger?'

'I'm beginning to think I got what you wanted, Chief.'

'Did you discover what happened to Ritchie?'

'Jagger was never interested in me, was he? It was you

who sent those thugs for me – you used the name Scorpio to get me hooked.'

Thorn sighed and sat on the bed, her eyes narrowing as she spoke.

'I was desperate, Astrid. The fight against organised crime is unrelenting and impossible to win. Today, low-level organised crime is what's most visible here. London is a playground for smash-and-grab robbers, petty thieves, and gangsters seeking to expand their territory and yields throughout the city, often at a terrible human cost. Other more profitable activities are better hidden, and that's what we're struggling against.'

Astrid stared at her. 'It's always been this way, Jude – you know this.'

Thorn dug her fingers into the bedsheet.

'It's different now. Most UK organised crime operates all but unchecked because there's so much of it and not enough people to deal with it. Over five thousand criminal gangs and syndicates in Britain employ nearly forty thousand professional gangsters. An ancient and fragmented structure of forty-three English and Welsh county forces, some of which date back almost two hundred years, has left us with little to no capability to respond to modern global criminals.

'Britain has become the hub for organised international crime, for traffickers of drugs, guns and people; a haven for fraudsters, cyber-criminals, money launderers and gangs of groomers and child abusers. We're trying to tackle 21st-century global crime with police officers deployed according to a 19th-century arrangement.'

Astrid saw the despair in her face and heard it in her voice. 'You need to modernise.'

Thorn shook her head. 'Cuts and under-funding have

made the police irrelevant. As a result, serious and organised criminals can swan around this city thinking they're above the law, while organised crime harms more people than terrorism. Globalisation and technology have allowed professional criminals to evolve into an international trillion-dollar giant of shifting alliances and ever-adapting enterprises – and Britain is the centre for all of it.

'We – the police – can't keep up with all of this. Progressive change needs to be driven across a fragmented system, but the police in Britain are riven by a closed archaic macho system resistant to change and social progression. We need wholesale reform and more funding, but alas, I don't think we'll ever get it.'

'Where does Paul Jagger come into all of this?'

Thorn slipped off the bed. 'After ten years, we've got nothing concrete on him, and I know he had Ritchie killed. So I'd given up hope when you strode into the station to report your sister missing.'

'And that's when you had the bright idea to include me in your desperation?'

'It came to me in a flash as soon as I saw you. We would never get Jagger through legal methods, but you, Astrid Snow; I knew you could do it.'

'What are you talking about?'

'Don't be modest, Astrid. I know you joined the Agency after you jumped ship on Ramon's little criminal gang. How else would you have escaped a long prison sentence for hacking GCHQ?'

'I could break your neck for using me like this, Jude.'

'Or you could give me what you got from Jagger's mansion.'

'You mean this?' Astrid held the USB stick in front of her. 'I might flush this down the toilet.'

The Chief Inspector shook her head. 'What's on it?'

'I broke the law to get this. Doesn't that bother you?'

Thorn's eyes burnt into her. 'It's too late for that, Astrid. What's on the drive?'

'It's full of videos of Jagger hurting women. He claimed it was all consensual, but I doubt it.'

'Is DC Ritchie in any of the clips?'

'I don't know. I haven't checked them all.'

Thorn held out her hand. 'Are you going to give it to me?'

Astrid shrugged. 'Why should I after you deceived me? What would have happened if I'd gone with those thugs to the pub to see the non-existent Mr Scorpio?'

'I knew you wouldn't. You're not someone who bows down to demands, especially from strange blokes on the street.'

'Why didn't you just ask me to meet Jagger and search his place?'

'Would you have done that?'

Astrid peered deep into her eyes. 'Does he have anything to do with Courtney and Olivia's disappearance?'

'I don't know.'

The USB drive was light in Astrid's fingers, a flimsy piece of plastic containing terrible things.

'You're keeping something from me, Jude.' She moved towards the bathroom. 'Last chance before this goes into the sewer.'

The room was silent for thirty seconds before Thorn spoke.

'DC Ritchie's undercover work in Jagger's empire was known only to me and one other, a trusted Detective Inspector. Ritchie would contact us using a secret email account. In one of her messages, she mentioned how she'd overheard Jagger's lieutenants talking about a woman inter-fering with their operation. So they spoke about how to deal with her.'

Astrid took a deep breath. 'Courtney?'

Thorn shook her head. 'The name in Ritchie's message was Vanessa Moore.'

She dropped the USB drive on the floor, grabbed Thorn's jacket and pulled the Chief Inspector towards her.

'You knew this and kept it from me. Then you tricked me into meeting Jagger.'

'I was desperate. The police can't do anything against him, but I knew you could.'

She let go of Thorn and pushed her into the table. Astrid put her foot next to the USB drive, ready to crush it.

'You don't care if I break the law?'

'I'll do anything to get Jagger, just like you will to find your family.'

'What else did Ritchie say about Moore?'

'She said we had to protect her.'

'But you didn't, did you?'

'How could we? If we did, Jagger would have known we had an undercover officer in his operation.'

'Did you tell Ritchie you wouldn't protect Moore?'

'Of course. She had to focus on getting the evidence we needed to put Jagger behind bars.'

Astrid reached down and grabbed the USB drive.

'How long after that was it before Ritchie disappeared?'

Thorn puffed out her cheeks. 'Two days.'

Astrid clenched the data disk in her fist.

'Tell me what you know, or it won't be only this going into the bog.'

The Chief Inspector eyed the drive.

'Moore and your sister worked for a women's refuge.

My officers contacted the organisation several times, which is how I know they were also helping women out of trafficked prostitution.'

Astrid struggled for breath. 'Courtney did this?'

'Indeed. I still remember all the terrible things you said about her when you accused your father of hurting you. I guess she must have changed a lot over the years.'

'Do you know where they are?'

'Moore is part of some cult in Scotland. I'm guessing she took your sister and niece there. The group is called Vanguard.'

Astrid's heart pushed up against her ribs as she fought the urge to strangle Chief Inspector Jude Thorn there and then.

'You knew all this and kept it from me, just to get me into Jagger's mansion?'

'DC Ritchie is like a daughter to me. I need to find her. You were my best option for that.' She pointed at the USB drive in Astrid's hand. 'I have to know if I can use what's on there, and then question Jagger about her.'

'This cult, Vanguard – where in Scotland are they?'

'The Isle of Barra – do you know it?'

Astrid pushed past Thorn and grabbed her bag. Then she threw the USB drive on the bed.

'I will soon enough.'

She stepped out of the room, walked down the stairs, and left the hotel.

A cult? Courtney helping abused women?

It sounded more unbelievable by the second.

23   ASTRID RENTS A CAR

Astrid went straight from her hotel to rent a car. It was so long since she'd driven, she wasn't sure if her driving licence was still valid, but it had six months left on it. While she waited in the reception, she peered at the paper she'd found in Courtney's house.

Vanguard.

Had Vanessa Moore given Courtney the paper, letting her know where they'd be going to escape Paul Jagger's clutches? Was Jagger more involved in people trafficking than he'd let on? Or was he interested in Moore because of the alleged connection with the undercover police officer, Detective Constable Ritchie?

Astrid turned her free hand into a fist, thinking about how Thorn had lied and manipulated her. She blamed her inability to see the deception on being tired after returning from America, but she knew that was an excuse.

I've been lazy and arrogant since I got back.

She forced the fingernails into her palm, wanting to feel the pain run through the whole of her body to match what was inside her head. A pretty blonde woman smiled at her from behind the reception desk, but that wasn't enough to distract her from the anger she felt with herself. She peered at the paper again, moving past the text to see the phone number written in blood.

Should I call Ophelia and tell her the new information I have?

She thought long and hard about it as the smell of lemon air freshener drifted through the room. Ophelia had helped her deal with the Kabaks, but dragging her to Scotland wouldn't do her any favours if Kate Gregory was still in London. But Ophelia had said there was a connection between the teenage girl and Jagger. Which meant Ophelia had to confront Jagger, and while Astrid would like to help her with that, she had to get to Scotland now.

I'll sort things out in Scotland first. Then I'll come back to help Ophelia with Jagger.

She removed the mobile phone from her pocket and considered sending Ophelia a text to tell her what she was about to do, but then thought better of it.

She'd only want to come with me or follow me – it's safer if she stays here. Once I've discovered the truth about this Vanguard cult on the Isle of Barra, then I'll let her know what's happening.

So instead of messaging Ophelia, she opened the web browser and searched for Vanguard and cults. There were a lot of results, over five million, but the first few pages were all to do with an American cult called NXIVM, whose leader had named himself "Vanguard". Astrid spent ten minutes reading several websites, learning how in 2017, a *New York Times* report inspired a justice department investigation that took down a multi-level marketing scheme turned "sex cult". The organisation had been operating for two decades under the guise of offering self-help deprogramming to heiresses, Hollywood actors, and influential CEOs. But, after a survivor came forward, someone exposed it as a group abusing its members emotionally and physically.

Astrid took a deep breath, removed the headphones from her pocket and attached them to the phone. Then she watched and listened to survivors of the cult speaking about their experiences, with interview footage from many once high-ranking inner-circle members of NXIVM. Her heart sank with every word she heard, her mind possessed of images of Olivia somehow being involved with something as terrible as this.

Then she shook the thoughts from her head – NXIVM was broken up when its leaders were imprisoned in 2020; plus, it was on the other side of the world. Moore, Courtney, and Olivia couldn't be caught up in something like that.

Could they?

Yet, Thorn had said Vanguard was a cult – and the word was on the paper Moore must have given Courtney. Perhaps it had been the only way out and away from Jagger and his crime empire.

Astrid read more about NXIVM, how the leader and the women closest to him twisted self-improvement into self-blame – members were taught there were no victims, that you could never be victimised. She examined how groups like NXIVM are formed and how people get hooked into them: it isn't about cults, but abuses of power that can happen anywhere in many organisations – even in families.

She was thinking about Olivia when the pretty blonde approached and waved a set of car keys at her. Astrid removed the headphones to hear what she was saying.

'A Peugeot 208, just like you asked for, Ms Snow.' As she handed her the keys, the woman brushed her finger against Astrid's hand. 'Rented for a week, and I'll be here waiting for you when you get back.'

She returned the woman's smile, for once incapable of flirting with so many terrible thoughts pouring through her mind.

'I promise to return it in one piece,' Astrid said.

The woman smiled again and showed her the car. Astrid followed her outside, her stomach rumbling to remind her she hadn't eaten for a while. She didn't know how long it would take to get to Barra, but it was obvious she needed to eat before she did. She thanked the pretty blonde, making a mental note of her smile before getting into the car and driving to the nearest fast food joint.

She sipped on a Coke and let the burger linger in her mouth as she continued reading about cults. Astrid had dealt with plenty of criminal organisations while working for the Agency, but most of those were driven by money or power. A few were based on warped ideologies, but they tended to be ones that wanted to promote violent world-views. From what she read online as she tucked into the junk food, cults were all about manipulating people to control them using a range of brainwashing techniques. Victims were gaslighted, demoralised, sleep-deprived, put on starvation diets, isolated from their friends and families, and subjected to scientifically dubious forms of psychotherapy.

Astrid peered out of the window, focused on Courtney and Vanessa Moore.

Had they gone to this cult because it was the only place far away enough to be out of Jagger's reach? Or had one or both of them always been a member of this Vanguard group?

Courtney in a cult is more believable than my sister

helping people. Her warped devotion to Lawrence was like worshipping a cult leader.

She thought about her time in the Agency, of all the moments when she'd used some of those psychological controls when interviewing prisoners: sleep deprivation on terrorist suspects; separating them from everybody they knew, especially family. She'd manipulated their thinking until they'd given in and told the Agency – had told her – everything they'd wanted.

Astrid dumped the rubbish in the glove compartment and pushed the thoughts of cults out of her head to concentrate on something more practical – getting to the Isle of Barra. She opened the GPS on her phone and used Google Maps to plan the journey: a ten-hour drive to Oban, then five hours on the ferry to Castlebay. If she left now and drove straight there without stopping, she'd get to Oban for eight o'clock. Could she catch a ferry at that time? She checked the Hebridean and Clyde Ferries website and found that was a no – the last would leave just after one in the afternoon.

She gazed at the details, frustrated to have to wait longer to see Olivia, but knowing the Monday afternoon ferry was her best option. That would get her to Castlebay around six o'clock, and then it would be a short drive to Barra.

But where would this Vanguard group be?

She went back to the search she'd done earlier for Vanguard and cults, scrolling past all the ones about NXIVM, about to give up after ten pages of the same thing when she saw a link to a Reddit page mentioning Vanguard and a woman called Joanna Pearson. Astrid clicked on it and trawled through the first few posts. Unfortunately, there was very little actual information there. Instead, people moaned about what Pearson was trying to achieve – a place where women and girls could develop their creativity in a safe environment. That was it – one statement from an anonymous poster who claimed to have been a student when Pearson was a psychology professor at the University of Glasgow.

Astrid ignored the rantings of the angry men complaining about "sexual apartheid" and opened another browser to search for Joanna Pearson. She saw links for an author, lawyer, athlete and even a model – but no academic. So she tried the University of Glasgow website, but with the same results – nothing.

She pushed her spine into the seat, frustrated again because she'd thought she'd found something useful, only to have it swept away from her once more.

Was it all just a fake to wind up those on the Reddit site?

She rested the phone on her lap, a feeling sweeping through her that she was getting closer to finding Olivia and Courtney while also moving further away from them. The text on the screen was unfolding before her eyes, turning into a scrambled spaghetti version of how confused she was. It was the obvious ramblings of those who didn't get out much, but the poster who'd claimed to be Pearson's psychology student at the University of Glasgow intrigued Astrid.

People claiming to be gurus and spiritual leaders were nothing new. Still, the internet and social media had helped with their prevalence and ability to collect followers with ease. If it was true about Pearson and she was the leader of this Vanguard, regardless of where she got the name, she wouldn't be the first failed academic to reinvent themselves as a guru for the disenfranchised.

And if Pearson had created a haven for women and girls, then Astrid was all for it.

Did Vanessa Moore know Pearson from her time in academia? If so, it would make sense for Moore to seek refuge in Pearson's Vanguard group, especially if it was in a place as remote as Barra. Astrid didn't think there would be much crime on the island, and nothing on a large-scale organised level.

Or perhaps Courtney met Pearson while she was at university. They would have been in different parts of the UK, but it is possible.

While she thought about that, Astrid bought her ferry ticket through the website. Then she booked a room for the night in Oban. She could think about searching Barra for Vanguard when she was in her hotel.

She reached across and turned the radio on, switched over to Bluetooth and plugged her phone into the car. The GPS directions were already set for Oban – all she needed now was a ten-hour music playlist to keep her going and focus her mind.

As she pulled out of the car park, Paul McCartney started singing about all of his troubles being so far away. She drove towards hers, hoping it wouldn't be long before she was reunited with Olivia.

And if Courtney was part of this Vanguard cult?

Well, the one thing Astrid knew how to do more than anything else was break away from those controlling you.

24 ASTRID CROSSES THE SEA

George Harrison was singing about his weeping guitar when Astrid parked outside the hotel in Oban. Her legs were stiff from the constant driving, her stomach craving sustenance while her bladder needed a trip to the toilet. She slung her bag over her back and stepped through the entrance. She checked in and dumped her stuff in the room, avoiding the temptation to go straight to the shower, instead returning downstairs and heading to the bar. She bought a large glass of wine and ordered steak before sitting in the corner and removing her phone. The place was empty, so at least she wouldn't have to wait long for the food.

She used the time to check for information about the Isle of Barra, downing half of her drink as she read about the garden of the Hebrides. The population was just over a thousand, eleven miles long and six miles wide. A single-track road ran around the coast of the southern part, following the flattest land and serving its coastal settlements. The interior was hilly and uninhabited, while the west and north contained white sands created from marine shells. The southeast side had several rocky inlets, and to the north, a sandy peninsula reached the beach airport and Eoligarry.

It sounded like the perfect place for some peace and quiet.

Astrid stared at the map of Barra, already wondering if she should have ordered a bottle and not a glass of wine.

I need a clear head for tomorrow.

She returned to the online information. Tourism was the main income for most islanders and they were still in the middle of the holiday season. Castlebay was the primary tourist base, with a few hotels, supermarkets, banks, and petrol stations.

Would Pearson keep her Vanguard close to the facilities or head somewhere more remote?

'Do you want any sauces with your steak?' A young woman in a hotel uniform put the plate on Astrid's table.

'Mustard if you have it,' Astrid said.

The woman nodded, giving Astrid the cutlery. She returned with the mustard as Astrid peered at images of the island on her phone.

'Are you going to Barradise Island for a holiday?'

She squeezed mustard over her steak as she stared at the server. 'Barradise Island?'

The woman laughed. 'That's what some of us call it – that or Barradise Lost.'

Astrid laughed with her. 'Do you know it well?'

'Born and bred there,' the woman said. 'Twenty-five years and I've never been further from it than this hotel. So if you need to know anything, just ask.'

Astrid didn't hesitate. 'Is there a women's refuge there called Vanguard?'

The server scrunched up her face. 'I'm not sure about the name, but there was a group who moved out to the deserted village about six months ago. I think they were all women and children.'

The strength of the mustard bit into the back of Astrid's throat and she had to wash it away with wine before she could speak.

'Deserted village?'

The woman glanced across the room, saw nobody around, and sat next to Astrid.

'It's called Balnabodach, a small township on the east side of Barra. People hadn't lived there since the end of the nineteenth century, but about a decade ago, developers built holiday cottages. I think somebody bought most or all of them last year. So that's where this group went, but I don't know who they are. They keep themselves to themselves, and it's easy to do out there.'

Isolation and solitude, miles away from any prying eyes – the perfect place to manipulate and control people.

Astrid thanked her, slipping her a five-pound note as a tip. And she ordered a bottle of wine. She crunched through a chunky chip as she searched for Balnabodach online, finding photos of the former holiday cottages the server had mentioned.

It wasn't much to go on, but it was a start.

Astrid smiled at the woman as she brought the bottle to the table. Then she finished the steak and ordered a dessert – apple pie with ice cream. The booze warmed her lips as she gazed at the photos, seeing the remains of houses abandoned when Queen Victoria was on the throne, and then scrutinising the modern buildings which might just contain her niece and sister.

What if I've come all this way and they're not there?

She tried not to think of it too much, pouring another glass of wine while wondering what she'd do if Courtney and Olivia were on the island.

How would she convince her sister it wasn't good for Olivia if they were in this cult?

And who was Astrid to say it wasn't good for them if they were part of a group protecting and helping women and girls?

Would it be beneficial for Olivia to grow up in that environment?

With Courtney?

The sweetness of the alcohol played havoc with her senses. Still, she knew being this isolated, not only physically but emotionally, from the rest of the world wouldn't be good for Olivia. But she had no right to take her away from her mother.

That thought stuck with her as she read about Balnabodach's terrible history. In 1850, Barra and the other islands of the Outer Hebrides were in the midst of the potato famines. The results on an over-populated island were catastrophic. Food was in short supply and people died of starvation. Because of this, the then landlord of Barra – Colonel Gordon of Cluny – decided the only way to relieve himself of the problem was to clear a part of the population forcibly. Balnabodach was selected as one township to be cleared. Four hundred and fifty islanders were forced onto ships and sent to Canada with a promise of work that never materialised.

Astrid read the contemporary accounts, horrified at what had happened: people hunted down by dogs, bound and thrown onto ships like cattle, and then transported overseas where they were abandoned in rags on the quayside – this was the fate of hundreds of men, women and children.

One young woman was said to have been seized as she was milking the family cow in the fields by the loch. She was put on a boat with nothing but the clothes she was wearing.

The Barra contingent was nearly one-third of the estimated seventeen hundred people cleared from the colonel's lands in the Western Isles that year. It wasn't known how many survived the winter, but Gordon, who also had estates in Aberdeenshire, continued to flourish. His fortune had been boosted earlier by compensation from the British Government of nearly twenty-five thousand pounds for the six plantations he owned in the Caribbean island of Tobago, which had more than a thousand slaves.

She put the phone on the table, losing her appetite as more images of rich men hurting the less fortunate placed themselves alongside the other terrible sights inside her head.

Was this where Courtney and Olivia lived, in the middle of a cult surrounded by the worst of history? Astrid grimaced at the potential irony of her sister finding refuge in a place where many had been abused.

And all because she was helping trafficked women and girls get away from their captors.

She wished she had more information about Vanessa Moore to guide her judgement regarding how benign Moore was. But it wouldn't be the first time Astrid had heard of somebody appearing to be assisting people to escape from a horrible situation, only to trap them inside an even worse one.

But if her sister and niece lived in an idyllic community, how could she force them to return to London?

She removed the paper from her pocket, staring at the bloodstained phone number.

Ophelia Red wouldn't have any problems taking Olivia from Courtney. Perhaps I should have brought her with me.

Astrid let that thought linger in her head. She swallowed the wine as the server brought the apple pie and ice cream to the table. She took her time eating it, drinking slowly while a thousand and one permutations ran through her mind.

———

SHE CHECKED out at twelve the next day, forgoing breakfast or lunch, and drove straight to the ferry. The wind threatened to blow away the flags as she got onto the transport, cutting across her face as she left the car and went to the main deck. She had four hours and forty minutes ahead of her, so she settled in to watch the scenery.

They moved out of the port as smaller vessels sat in the water nearby. She checked her phone, wondering one last time if she should have phoned Ophelia. Then she thought about Chief Inspector Jude Thorn and what she would have found on that USB.

Perhaps I'll find something on Barra which helps convict Jagger.

A million other notions crawled at her brain as she connected the headphones to her ears and turned the music on. Bowie's pretty things were driving their parents' insane as Astrid focused on the journey's highlights: seeing Ben Nevis against the skyline; dolphins jumping in and out of the water as they swam alongside the ferry; plus the sight of Castlebay as they approached the island with the view of an ancient castle rising out of the water.

The wind and the sea were sweeping across her face as she arrived. She wiped them away as she returned to her car. A full moon was hanging in the sky as she drove onto the island. The road was empty, the ten-minute drive to Balnabodach uneventful, and the countryside spectacular, switching from wildflowers to expansive untouched beaches. It all seemed like the perfect holiday place to escape from everything. Under other circumstances, she might have been able to enjoy herself.

Maybe once I find Olivia and Courtney, I can relax.

She couldn't remember the last time she'd had a holiday. She'd visited America but, no matter how hard she'd tried, it had been impossible to turn that trip into a break – too many bodies had a way of piling up around her.

The cottages were easy to spot amongst the emptiness of the landscape, two smaller buildings with a much larger one behind them. There were two Land Rovers outside the nearest cottage as Astrid parked next to them. As she stepped out of the car, sea spray danced above the waves, lifted and twirled by the power of the wind. It skipped across her face, creating a chill that sparked her legs into life. She locked the car, tasting the salt in the air as a flock of gulls flew above her.

It was an early summer evening, but she knew she wasn't dressed for the conditions; her flimsy top, jacket and jeans wouldn't keep out the weather as it got darker. Even now, as she stared at the buildings, the wind was clawing at her clothes to tell Astrid how foolish she'd been not to wear something more sturdy.

She strode towards the building, the gravel crunching under her feet. The noise travelled through her, adding to the tension that gripped every part of her.

Courtney and Olivia are here, or they're not and I'll have to start all over again.

And if they were inside one of these buildings, she'd have to discover if they were in the grip of a cult or not.

Vanguard.

That word filled her head as she knocked on the door.

25 ASTRID HAS A CONVERSATION

A tall young woman opened the door, bending her head to smile at Astrid.

'We've been waiting for you. Please come in.'

Astrid didn't move. 'You know who I am?'

'Dr Pearson will explain everything. My name is Emma.'

She stood to the side so Astrid could see inside the entrance. Astrid stepped in, glad to find a bit of warmth away from the chill that had descended outside. Emma took her into a living room and the smells of burning wood and a fresh fire.

'Would you like a drink?' Emma said.

Astrid answered with her own question. 'Who do you think I am?'

'You're Astrid Snow. So how about that drink? We have alcohol.'

'Cider or wine – I'm easy.'

'Your reputation precedes you, Ms Snow.'

The words came from behind her. She turned to see a

woman, her long dark hair tied behind her as steely blue eyes bore into Astrid.

'Are you Joanna Pearson?'

The woman nodded. 'Dr Joanna Pearson at your service, Ms Snow.'

'Call me Astrid. What are you a doctor of?'

Pearson laughed. 'Anyone with a doctorate can be called Doctor. The doctor's degree was a product of the medieval universities; this higher degree simply conferred the right to teach. This "doctoring" verb made it easy to call medical practitioners "doctors".'

'And?'

'So, I'm a Doctor of Psychology.'

'Did you teach at the University of Glasgow?'

'I did, for five years.'

'There's no record of you on their website. In fact, there's not much of a record of you anywhere online.'

'I like to keep out of the public eye, and I think the university was happy to distance themselves from me.'

'Why is that?'

'All in good time,' Pearson said as she nodded to Emma.

Emma gave them both a glass of cider and Pearson indicated for Astrid to sit opposite her near the fire.

Astrid hugged the glass. 'What is this place, Dr Pearson?'

'Since we're on first-name terms, call me Joanna, and I'll answer all your questions to the best of my abilities.'

Astrid settled into the chair. A gremlin in her brain wondered if this was another trap and her drink had been drugged again. She ignored that voice and sipped at the dry apple taste.

'Are you renting the holiday cottages?'

Pearson shook her head. 'My foundation bought all three buildings.'

'Why is your foundation here?'

'We needed the isolation to grow and develop far from the restraints of the modern patriarchal world.'

'There are no men here?'

'Only young boys, along with the rest of the children. We have our own school, where the children are taught to treat people with compassion and kindness.'

'Does the government know about this?'

'It's been sanctioned at the highest level.'

Astrid sighed. 'I guess I'm not surprised. Imagine the degree of conditioning you can instil out here, where you're remote enough to keep out of sight of the authorities and Ofsted.'

'Don't be so cynical, Astrid. All education is conditioning. Little boys and girls have had their roles instilled into them for centuries, the same for the working classes and those deemed worthy of existing only on the lowest strata of society. There are no class distinctions here, no gender roles, and no racial divisions.'

'You're trying to create Utopia.'

Pearson laughed. 'No, not quite. We're aiming to make humanity better, even if it's only a small part of it. Don't you think that's worth attempting?'

'Sure, but you're setting people up for a lifetime of hurt when they leave this island and enter the big, wide world. What do you expect your converts to do when they meet the savages of the civilised society?'

Pearson ignored the jab. 'I hope they'll be good people, nothing more, nothing less.'

'Speaking of which, where are my sister and niece?'

Pearson's shoulders slumped for a microsecond. 'Courtney doesn't want to see you.'

Astrid wasn't surprised. And didn't care. That wasn't why she'd travelled this far.

'But she is here?'

'Yes,' Pearson said.

'What about Olivia?'

'She's unaware of your presence here.'

Astrid dug the nails into her palms and controlled her breathing. 'Why?'

'It may be prudent if you wait a while and I'll talk to your sister. We have plenty of spare rooms; you can use one of those. And our chef is the best on the island.'

'How do you know who I am?' Astrid said.

Pearson sipped at her cider. 'A member of our community works at the hotel at Oban. Once she saw an Astrid Snow had booked a room, she guessed you might be related to Courtney.'

Astrid laughed. 'My sister must have been thrilled at the news.'

Pearson smiled at her. 'Blood families can be difficult at times. I have my experience with this.'

'Blood families? What other types of families are there?'

Pearson lifted a hand to her face and Astrid noticed the difficulty she had moving her fingers.

'The families we make with friends, the ones not based on blood or genetics. My childhood unfolded within a community that believed sharing the rearing of children between all the adults was more productive than relying on birth parents.'

Astrid considered how it might have been for her if she'd been raised by somebody other than Lawrence and her mother.

'And how did that work out for you?'

Pearson smiled at her. 'It was an education.'

Astrid relaxed a little, the ache in her bones from the torturous journey refusing to leave every inch of her. And she needed to eat again.

There's a worm in my guts.

'Where did you get all the money for this? Does academia pay so well nowadays?'

Pearson put her drink down and Astrid saw the marks on her hand again. She must have seen her staring at it.

'An injury when I was a teenager quite a long time ago.' She glanced at the window. 'It was on land not too dissimilar to this, but not as remote. At least not physically.' She touched her head, and then her heart. 'But it was in these places. I grew up in a disciplined community. When I was a child, my parents were removed from the community for physical and emotional cruelty against me. What I didn't know until it was too late was they were still in contact with the leader of our group, and he passed on my newborn daughter to them.'

Astrid recognised the pain consuming her face. 'What happened?'

'I left, searching for the family I needed and the one I didn't. When I caught up with my parents, they were already wealthy from manipulating the stock market. So when they died, I inherited their wealth.'

'And your daughter?'

'I never found her. My mother and father wouldn't tell me what they did with her, and the police weren't interested. My parents were generous contributors to the local community, you see. Even after they died, I kept on looking, but it was no use. So I took their money and got myself a proper education, rising through the ranks to get my doctorate.'

'Why did you leave the University of Glasgow? Was it because of this Vanguard?'

'It was partly that,' Pearson said. 'But my so-called superiors at the university weren't happy with what I was trying to teach my students.'

Astrid drank more of the cider. 'And what was that?'

'Isn't it obvious? We need a radical change to education and beyond. Whole curriculums and educational structures have to be scrapped so we can teach our children, especially boys, that empathy and compassion are more important than anything else. We must work as a collective to make the world a better place. Empathy and compassion can be taught to those who appear to lack them. The age-old debate of nature versus nurture is false. It takes both to construct individual personality. Bad people are not born that way; they're made. Therefore, education is so important at all points in life, especially in the earliest stages of childhood. It's more imperative for a child to understand ethics and morality than maths and science.'

'So who chooses what is moral and ethical?'

'Those are universal traits. Only those with warped personalities would view torture, suffering and murder as moral.'

'I've met those types of people, many of them, and I'm telling you, empathy can't be taught. You either have it or you don't.'

'You don't believe in rehabilitation?'

'It's not the same thing. Criminals can be shown why their actions are bad, but it doesn't mean they'll empathise with their victims. Some may even appear sorry for what they've done, but in reality, they're sad for themselves, not others. And what about violent acts committed during warfare or in defending people from violence or abuse?'

'But that's the whole point, Astrid. If we, as teachers, get it right from the earliest childhood years, then we won't have to protect anybody from violence or abuse because those things won't exist. And there'll certainly be no need for large-scale conflicts or wars.'

Astrid shook her head. 'You're trying to create a Utopia. You're not the first to attempt it, and I admire your conviction, but it's never going to happen – not here on this island or anywhere else.'

'While I respect your opinion, you haven't been here long enough to form such a judgement. So why don't you stay with us for a bit on the island? If nothing else, you'll get to embrace the wonders of nature here.'

Why not? Nothing is waiting for me in London.

'You have the room?'

Pearson finished her drink. 'Come with me and I'll show you.'

She got up as Astrid drank the rest of her cider before following Pearson through the door at the back. They stepped through a kitchen and went outside. The larger structure Astrid had seen earlier was opposite them.

She spoke to Pearson as the older woman led her into the building.

'Why take the name Vanguard?'

Pearson grinned at her. 'A group of people leading the way in new developments and ideas. Doesn't that sound like what we're doing here?'

'It was also a name used by a cult leader in an organisation called NXIVM. Are you aware of that?'

She shook her head. 'I've never heard of them. But I

think it's appropriate for a community trying to develop human thinking and behaviour.'

'Vanguard also means the foremost part of an advancing force.'

Pearson's laugh echoed off the walls. 'You think that's us?' She clutched at her chest. 'When Courtney said you were cynical, I didn't realise it was this much.'

Astrid stopped. 'What else did she say about me?'

Pearson pursed her lips. 'Oh, not a lot. She said you talked little.'

'Is Olivia okay?'

'She is. We have plenty of kids her age to teach here.'

'And indoctrinate.' It wasn't a question.

Pearson ignored her words. 'Follow me, Astrid Snow.'

They took a sharp right and went into a large room. Two women supervised a dozen children as the kids covered the walls and themselves in paint. Astrid's heart leapt when she saw Olivia painting a giant pink cat on the wall. She strode past everyone else and approached her niece.

Perhaps she's forgotten about me.

Olivia turned and quashed that thought in an instant.

'Aunty Astrid!'

She dropped the paintbrush and threw her arms around Astrid's waist. Nothing would ever replace the joy that rushed through Astrid then. When Olivia pulled away, pink paint stuck to Astrid's trousers and jacket. She bent her knees and reached down to Olivia's level.

'How've you been, kid?'

Olivia's smile was bright enough to recharge Astrid's weary bones.

'It's great here, Aunty Astrid. They have toys and games and animals to pet and other kids and everything.'

She was a balloon ready to pop. Astrid pulled her niece to her and hugged her again. Then she let go and got up.

'Where's your mother, Olly?'

The kid's smile didn't fade. 'She's off somewhere with Nessa.'

Nessa?

'Vanessa Moore?'

'No one calls her that, Aunty Astrid. It's Nessa.'

Olivia grabbed the brush and returned to her artwork. Astrid took a long breath, stood, and turned to Pearson.

'I need a shower and something to eat. Then I'll speak to my sister.'

And maybe my head might have cleared by then.

26 ASTRID'S FAMILY REUNION

An hour later, Astrid was sitting in one of the largest libraries she'd ever seen. Wall to wall books surrounded her. She resisted the urge to browse the collection, still feeling the warmth of Olivia's arms around her. The paint had dried on her clothes, the smell keeping the moment of their reconnection burning in her memory. She needed it there as a barrier against how she felt about the upcoming reunion with her sister.

After Astrid's shower, Emma had returned to show her around. She didn't see Olivia again, but saw a group of six other children, including two young boys, being taught English by a woman in a small room. On her journey through the house, she observed groups of women involved in various activities: baking bread, fixing computers, repairing a broken wall – even making alcohol. She could understand why this place would help people, but she couldn't see it as a long-term answer to society's problems as Pearson claimed it could be.

That's if what she told me was true.

Astrid glanced at the books again, her gut craving more

booze while her head sought answers for why her sister had come here.

She's working with Vanessa Moore to get women away from abusive relationships and to safety in Pearson's New Utopia.

If it weren't so ludicrous, she'd have cracked up laughing. Courtney Snow, the girl who spent years encouraging their father to abuse Astrid. And who smiled while she watched him do it. Now she was helping others escape violence.

She was considering her sister's unlikely conversion when Vanessa Moore walked into the library. She looked older than in the photos Astrid had seen on Facebook, her face darkened by great shadows and bags under her eyes. Courtney followed in behind Moore, hair cut short to resemble Mia Farrow in her youth.

'Why are you here?' There was no emotion in her sister's voice.

Astrid returned the coldness. 'I'm worried about Olivia.'

Courtney's shoulders shook as she laughed, a terrifying sight that transported Astrid back to her teens and another beating from her father as her sister watched.

'There's no need for you to worry about my daughter.'

'Why did you bring her here? You've uprooted Olivia from her home, friends, and school to drag her six hundred miles to what?' Astrid glanced around the room. 'It's a good idea for her to read more, but this is extreme.'

Courtney glared at her. 'Why do I have to explain myself to you?'

The sun was disappearing outside the window, but the shiver running through Astrid wasn't to do with the temperature change.

'I'm concerned about you being a responsible human

being. You couldn't do it as a sister, so you're highly unlikely to do it now as a mother.'

Courtney lunged at Astrid, but Moore pulled her back.

'What right do you have to talk to me like this?' She snarled at Astrid like a caged animal. 'You're the one who ruined our family. You don't get to tell me how to raise my child.'

Astrid peered at her, seeing more emotion in her than she'd done before. Even when Lawrence was raining his fists down on his younger daughter, Courtney would watch on unemotionally. At first, Astrid had thought it was because she was afraid of him and worried he'd harm her as well. But she soon learnt it was because her sister had encouraged Lawrence to hurt Astrid and enjoyed watching it happen. Her smile was there, small and curled up along her top lip – somewhat hidden as if she didn't want to waste it all on the person she hated so much.

'This is why I don't trust you with Olivia, Courtney – you haven't changed since you were encouraging him to abuse me.'

'What?' Moore said.

Astrid laughed without feeling happy.

'Hasn't she told you what she did to me, Vanessa? That's hardly a surprise, but it might explain my reluctance to trust her with Olivia; or to believe she's been helping you rescue trafficking victims.'

Moore held Courtney's hand. 'I don't know what happened between you and your sister, Ms Snow, but I've seen what a good mother she is. And she has helped me get dozens of women and girls away from the most terrible abuse and sexual exploitation.' She smiled at Courtney. 'Whatever she was like when you were kids isn't who she is now.'

Astrid couldn't believe what she'd heard, slumping into a sofa to take the weight off her legs and from her brain.

'Tell me about this trafficking gang you infiltrated.'

Courtney let go of Moore's hand. 'You don't need to tell her anything, Nessa.'

Moore patted Courtney's fingers as if she was a child.

'I didn't infiltrate anything, Ms Snow. Instead, I saw a young girl, Sarah, outside my school one day – not one of our kids – and got talking to her. It was obvious she was in trouble, but she was reluctant, or too scared, to tell me about it. But I saw her again, and, over time, she opened up to me until I discovered what was wrong.'

'Where was her family?' Astrid said.

'She didn't have one,' Moore replied. 'She was an only child, and her parents had died in a car crash three years before. After that, she slipped into the care system, shoved between pillar and post, never finding a single person with her best interests at heart. Eventually, she was groomed into prostitution; initially by a teenage boy she met before being passed on to older men as if she was a piece of meat from the butcher's.'

Moore stopped talking, and Astrid recognised the anger in her eyes as it matched her own.

'Did you go to the police?' Astrid said.

The teacher put one hand on her heart and laughed.

'Of course. And where do you think that got me?'

Astrid sank further into the sofa, expecting it to swallow her whole.

'Nowhere.'

Moore nodded. 'Sarah had been abused before, in care, and the authorities hadn't believed her then. And the police didn't either when I went to them. You would have thought with the number of high-profile grooming cases in the media in recent years, they would have at least investigated her claims. But, to them, she was only one girl with a troublesome history, and they had more important things to do with their valuable time.'

'So you took measures into your own hands?' Astrid said.

'I had to, but it's not as easy as just removing the victims from their abusers – you have to think of where they can go and what the consequences might be from the criminals.' She smiled at Courtney. 'Luckily, I knew someone who was already helping at a charity, and she worked at the same place as me.'

Astrid's head jerked forward in shock.

'Courtney?' She looked at her sister as if she'd never seen her before. 'What charity was that? The Ayn Rand school for gifted children?'

Courtney's glare had vanished, replaced with that cruel smile Astrid had experienced so many times.

'You know nothing about me, Astrid, and you never did.'

Astrid sprang from the chair, ready to strangle her sister and only stopping when Joanna Pearson walked into the room.

'Vanessa was my student at university and we kept in touch over the years.' She smiled at them, but it did little to quell the fire burning through Astrid's veins. 'Once she told me what was happening, it only accelerated the plans I had for an environment like this one.'

'Vanguard?' Astrid said. Pearson nodded. 'Are all the women here escaping from abusive relationships?'

Pearson peered deep into Astrid's soul. 'I guess so.'

Astrid couldn't control herself, the laughter bursting from her like an exploding volcano.

'How well do you know my sister, Dr Pearson?'

Pearson moved beyond the books towards Courtney and Vanessa.

'I've seen nothing but kindness in the short time I've known her. And, for your information, Courtney was working with disadvantaged children when I first met her. So whatever was in the past between you is best left there. I'm not one of those psychologists who believe dredging up the past helps anybody deal with their present or progress into the future.'

Astrid sat there unmoving, her body as frozen as her brain. Was Vanguard a cult and Pearson manipulating them all, including her sister? Or was Courtney really a changed person, doing good and helping others?

Is this her redemption for what she did to me? For what she allowed to happen to me?

'What do you plan to do now?' Astrid said.

Pearson moved to the bookcase and removed one volume, a large book about the benefits of working as a community compared to the selfishness of individuals.

'Do you know some of the history of this island, Astrid?'

She took a deep breath, glad to be talking about something other than the complex history between Courtney and her.

'I read about some rich landowner in the nineteenth century who forced hundreds of islanders, including women and children, out of their homes and to sail to Canada. He'd promised them a new life, a better one, but that was a lie, and they landed only to find poverty, homelessness and starvation.'

Pearson returned the book to the shelf. 'Indeed, that was the fate of the poor unfortunates who were forcibly cleared from the estates of Colonel John Gordon of Cluny. People were seized and dragged on board the ships. Men who resisted were felled with truncheons and handcuffed. Those who escaped, including some who swam ashore from a ship, were chased by the police or hunted down by dogs and returned to the ships. Gordon would be dead eight years after these tragic proceedings, but the damage had been done by this wealthy landowner and former Member of Parliament.'

'It's one of many horrific historical events hidden from the public, Joanna, but why are you telling me this?'

'Those terrible crimes were committed near to where we are sitting over a hundred and seventy years ago, yet the only people who recognised them as crimes at the time were those who suffered from them. So in the eyes of the law, they weren't crimes but lawful actions by the rightful owner of the land we're currently on. *Plus ça change, plus c'est la même chose*, Astrid.'

Astrid scrutinised her. 'The more things change, the more they stay the same.'

Pearson nodded. 'You of all people know how brutal this world can be, especially to its most sensitive citizens – and a lot of that brutality is waved away by the authorities and our political leaders, justified by their obsession with economics and ideologies. So all I and the others are doing is trying to help some of those who suffer the most.'

'What do you mean, me of all people?' Astrid said.

The psychologist glanced at Courtney and Moore before returning her gaze to Astrid.

'Every member of Vanguard has access to my professional experience.'

Astrid laughed again. 'You had a therapy session with my sister?'

She looked away from Pearson, seeing Courtney with her head lowered.

'We've had more than one meeting and, while what we discussed is private and confidential, I will say that she spoke about her family – and you in particular – quite a lot.'

Astrid couldn't speak, peering at the books behind Pearson and watching them spin around like a tormented kaleidoscope containing all of her past, telling her that everything she ever knew was now upside down and the wrong way round.

Finally, when her head stopped rotating, she was ready to talk to her sister. Astrid's reply was hanging on her lips when Emma burst into the room.

'There are two cars of men outside demanding to be let in. They're carrying guns.'

27 ASTRID'S SACRIFICE

ourtney scowled at her. 'After all we've done, and
then you lead them here.'

Astrid got up, ignoring her sister and addressing Emma.
The young woman's eyes were darting all over the place as
if she was searching for somewhere to hide.

'There are men outside with guns?'

Emma nodded. 'They're not from the island. They say
they're coming inside.'

Astrid glanced at the door and window.

'For two cars, that means there are ten of them at the
most. They might be abusive husbands or partners, but I
doubt they'll charge in here, even with those weapons.' She
turned to Pearson. 'They're trying to scare you, so you'll go
outside.'

'You haven't got any brighter with age, have you?'
Courtney said. She looked at the woman who'd delivered
the news. 'Bring the others here, Emma.'

Emma ran out as Astrid approached her sister. 'What's
going on?'

Vanessa Moore stepped between them. 'Jagger and his men must have followed you.'

Jagger? Has he come here for the videos I copied? Why hasn't Thorn used them to arrest him?

She looked at Moore. 'Paul Jagger? You're aware of his criminal activities?'

Moore nodded. 'I know who he is.'

'Is this to do with him trafficking women?' Astrid didn't wait for an answer, turning instead to Pearson. 'You call the police and I'll stall him.'

Pearson shook her head. 'He'll have paid them off, just like he has in London. And he's here for her.'

Astrid turned as Emma returned with a teenage girl and a woman, people she recognised from two photos: Detective Constable Ritchie and Kate Gregory.

DC Ritchie's sea-blue eyes pierced Astrid's gaze. 'I had to take Kate from him. In his human trafficking empire, he keeps a few for himself. My requests for help from my superiors went unheeded, no matter how many times I asked.'

'That was Chief Inspector Thorn?' Astrid said.

'You know her?' Ritchie said.

Astrid rechecked the door and window, expecting an intrusion even though she'd convinced herself the goons with guns would wait for her.

'Courtney and I go back a long way with Jude.'

She glanced at her sister, waiting for the penny to drop.

'What? Is that the bitch you spilt your guts to about Dad?'

Astrid ignored her and returned to DC Ritchie. 'Does Thorn know you're here?'

Could those men outside have anything to do with Thorn? She's played me once – might she have done it again? She was the one who told me Olivia and Courtney were here.

'No. I left my undercover work and didn't contact Thorn or the police. I couldn't sit back and let Jagger get his hands on Kate. I knew Vanessa and Courtney from their time with the women's refuge, and they convinced me to bring Kate here.' She looked at them. 'We thought it would be the last place he'd look for us.'

That's until I led him and his thugs here.

Courtney stepped towards her, a crescendo of hate blazing from her eyes.

'Are you happy, coming here and telling me how to raise my daughter? Now you've got all of us killed, including Olivia.'

Astrid ignored the words. She'd found it difficult dealing with her sister's unexpected change into a decent human being, and seeing Olivia always troubled her heart, but this was familiar ground to her. She turned to Emma.

'Are they still outside the building, the one I went into earlier?'

Emma nodded. 'They were two minutes ago.'

'And you're sure they're not locals or people from Oban? Or tourists?'

Courtney laughed at her. 'What holidays do you take where the tourists have guns?'

You have no idea, sister.

'They're not from here or anywhere close by,' Emma said.

'There isn't another ferry due until tomorrow, so could they have been on the same one as me? Then they waited and followed me here.'

Courtney threw up her hands. 'You led them right to us.'

'They might have flown into the island,' Pearson said.

'I'd imagine somebody as rich as Jagger wouldn't be patient enough to drive from London to here.'

'Yes,' Astrid said. 'That makes sense. But if he came via a different route to me, how did he know I was here?'

Did Thorn tell him I was coming here? Is this all part of her plan?

Courtney was staring daggers at her. 'Don't you try to kid us all this isn't to do with you.'

It's something to do with me, but I'm not sure what.

She ignored her sister's attack. 'How many people are in these buildings?'

Pearson arched her eyebrows. 'Including the kids, about thirty residents.'

More than enough to deal with Jagger and his goons. As long as they were up for fighting, which she assumed they weren't. But she wasn't on her own.

'Did you bring a weapon with you, DC Ritchie?'

The undercover officer lowered her eyes before raising them to look at Person.

'Joanna, you'll probably kick me out of here when this is over, but yes, I have a pistol in my room.'

Astrid breathed a sigh of relief. 'Let's survive this before we talk about anybody being kicked back to London.' She glanced at Courtney, and then back to DC Ritchie. 'And you have bullets, I hope?'

'About two dozen,' Ritchie said.

'You better use them sparingly, then.' Astrid turned to her sister and Moore. 'Are you up for protecting Olivia, Kate, and everyone else?'

Courtney pushed her face into Astrid, the closest they'd been since they were teenagers living under the same terrible roof.

'Who put you in charge? You're the one to blame for all of this.'

Pearson grabbed Courtney and dragged her away. 'Something tells me your sister has dealt with situations like this before.'

Everybody stared at Astrid, but it was Courtney who spoke.

'What, my little sister knows how to handle herself now?'

Astrid needed to stay calm, to prepare herself for the situation. Ever since Emma had burst into the room with the bad news, her hyperactive brain had spent half the time talking to the others and half trying to plan a way out of this mess.

'I never thought I'd say this, Courtney, but you're right. Somehow, those men followed me here, which is all my fault. But I promise you and everybody else I'll get all of us out of this safe and sound.' She gazed into her sister's eyes. 'Even you.' She took a deep breath. 'Though I'll be doing it for Olivia and the others, not for you.'

Courtney laughed at her. 'And how are you going to do that?'

'Are there any other weapons in the buildings?' Astrid said.

Vanessa spoke. 'We have a bunch of garden tools in storage, shovels and spades. We could use those.'

Emma stepped forward. 'And I can help as well.'

Astrid stared at her. 'How so?'

The young woman smiled at her. 'I'm a black belt in karate and do kickboxing every week. It's a class we teach in the Vanguard.'

Astrid looked at Pearson. 'Perhaps it's Utopia after all.'

'It will be,' Pearson said, 'as long as we survive this.'

Astrid scrutinised them, readying two escape maps in her head, one where she got everyone killed and one where she didn't.

Let's stick to the second map.

'Okay, great. If they have weapons, leave them to Ritchie and me.' She spoke to Moore. 'Go through the three buildings and make sure everybody is in a safe place. Keep the doors locked and don't open them unless it's Ritchie or I outside.' Then she spoke to her sister. 'Protect Olivia.' She didn't wait for a reply and addressed Pearson. 'Tell Jagger I'll be along to see him soon.'

Pearson left without questioning her instructions.

'Shall I get the gun?' Ritchie said.

'Yes, but keep it out of sight, so nobody here sees it. We don't want to spook anybody. Then bring it to me at the front.' Then she went to Kate Gregory, who was standing next to Moore. The kid didn't seem frightened, but Astrid guessed she must be. 'We haven't been properly introduced, Kate – I'm Astrid Snow.'

Kate beamed at her. 'I know all about you – you're Olivia's Aunty Astrid. She's always talking about you.'

Astrid glanced at Courtney, amused by the irritation on her sister's face.

'Well, Kate, you have me at a disadvantage since you know so much about me. Is it true you're Paul Jagger's step-niece?'

The teenager nodded. 'Mum told me not to see him, but I couldn't stay living with her, not with *him* there.'

Astrid didn't ask about *him*. 'Okay, Kate, but if we take you back to your mum and I get rid of *him* for you, will that be all right with you?'

'Yeah, I guess so,' Kate said. 'You can do that?'

Astrid touched the girl on the arm. 'I promise I will.'

Kate grabbed Astrid's hand and held it. 'Olivia was right about you – you are special.'

Then she let go and returned to Courtney and Moore. Astrid nodded to Emma, who led her and Ritchie out through the way Astrid had come earlier. As they marched along the corridor and past paintings of happy families and glorious landscapes, she peered again at the dried pink paint on her clothes. Then she wondered what Jagger was prepared to sacrifice for his perverted criminal life.

It was a brief walk out of the large building and into the smaller one in front of it. They found Pearson at the open doorway, gazing at the men in the cars. Astrid saw Jagger in the back of the closer vehicle.

'Have you spoken to him?' she said to Pearson.

'He's a man of few words.'

'Did you phone the police?'

'There's no answer.'

Astrid had expected it and knew it would have been pointless trying to use her mobile to call for help. So they were on their own with this.

She stepped out of the house. 'Are you stalking me, Paul?'

One of his goons wound down the car window.

'I owe you a great debt, Snow. I couldn't have found your sister without you.'

His thugs laughed in the background.

'Now you've had your day out and you should head back home, Paul. The Met will be waiting for you with open arms.'

The laughter continued. 'You don't think what you stole from me is enough for a prosecution, do you? I told you everything in those videos was consensual. I have signed documents to prove it.' He paused and the goons stopped laughing. 'Hand the girl over, and no one gets hurt.'

'The police are on their way, Jagger.'

His laugh returned. 'No, you know they're not, Snow. This is your last chance.'

Astrid turned from him to speak to Pearson. 'How secure are these buildings?'

'We're a community of helpers, not a prison.'

'Are most of the rooms secure?'

Pearson shook her head. 'There are locks on the residential suites, but they probably won't hold against a strong attack.'

DC Ritchie appeared behind them, showing Astrid the weapon tucked into her trousers.

'Hopefully, my sister and Vanessa have got everyone safe.' She spoke to Ritchie. 'Have you ever fired your gun?'

'Only in practice.'

'That'll have to do.' She focused on the cars again, watching Jagger waving his hand out the window. 'Do you need the toilet, Paul?'

'No more chances, Snow. My men will come in if I don't get what I want in thirty seconds.'

Astrid watched the car doors open, wondering who would make the biggest sacrifice in the next five minutes. Then she answered him.

'Send your thugs away and I'll give you the girl.'

28 ASTRID'S PROMISE

Ritchie gasped, but Pearson was unmoving, staring at Astrid through curious eyes. Then Jagger's tortured drawl broke the silence.

'Somehow, I don't trust you, Snow.'

Her reply was instant. 'I promise on my niece's life, I'll hand the girl to you, Paul.'

She couldn't say anything else before Ritchie pulled her into the house and pointed the gun in her face.

'You do and I'll shoot you.'

Astrid ignored the threat and spoke to Pearson. 'Do you trust me?'

Pearson scrutinised Astrid as Ritchie fumed. Then she nodded.

'I do.'

Ritchie let go of her, but kept the pistol aimed at Astrid.

Astrid returned outside. 'Do we have a deal, Paul?'

Jagger twitched in his seat. 'I'll send the other car away, and then you let two bodyguards and me inside for the girl. Do you agree?'

Astrid knew he didn't need to go into the house to get

Kate – he wanted to check the layout and see how many people were there.

'No. I'll bring the girl here for you. Send the car away and give me fifteen minutes. Okay?'

He nodded. 'Fifteen minutes and no more, Snow. After that, we're coming inside, and we won't be gentle.'

She stepped into the house, straight into the anger of the fuming detective constable.

'Give me the gun, June.'

Ritchie glared at her. 'You're joking. Your sister was right about you after all.' She lifted her arm and pointed the weapon at Astrid's face. 'I should shoot you now.'

'You could, but it will achieve nothing. If you trust me, I'll get all of us out of this mess. Can you do that, DC Ritchie?'

Pearson spoke before Ritchie could answer.

'One car has left.' She turned to look at them. 'Give her the gun, June. She'll deal with this.'

Ritchie hesitated for a second before handing over the weapon. Astrid slipped it into the back of her trousers.

'Now, let's see my sister.'

Ritchie shook her head and scowled. She led Astrid through the small house and towards the bigger one behind it. She stopped outside and faced Astrid.

'Are you really going to hand Kate over to him?'

'Don't you trust me?'

'I only met you a few hours ago.'

The detective constable scrutinised Astrid's face for a minute before stepping into the house. They went down a long corridor, and then upstairs, entering the first door. Astrid stared at a giant TV and a music centre, then glanced at the stack of CDs in the corner, surprised to find a rare Hoodlum Priest album there.

My copy disappeared twenty years ago.

She picked it up, opening the case to see that familiar scrawl of her teenage handwriting and her name.

Courtney stole it from me and kept it all this time?

She returned it to the pile and spoke to Ritchie.

'I don't let innocent people get hurt.'

'You're not God.'

'No, I'm not, but I share the desire for vengeance, and Jagger will pay for all the pain he's caused, I promise you that.'

'Just like you promised to give him Kate.'

She couldn't argue with that. 'The sooner you take me to her, the sooner this is over.'

Ritchie left without speaking and Astrid examined the rest of the room. Magazines were stacked in the corner, with pairs of walking boots and a laptop. Then she went to the CDs, resisting the urge to look again at the one her sister had stolen from her collection when they were teenagers. She was peering at it when Ritchie returned with Courtney, Vanessa, and Kate.

'Has he gone?' Moore said.

Astrid removed the gun from her trousers and placed it on a table.

'He will be soon, but I need to borrow Kate from you.'

The teenager flinched at the mention of her name and Courtney shook her head.

'You're going to sacrifice her to save yourself, aren't you, sister?' The head-shaking continued and Astrid expected it to fall off her shoulders. 'You haven't changed at all.'

Against her better judgment, and even though she didn't have the time for it, she argued with her sister.

'Unlike you, Courtney, who appear to have undergone a transformation of Damascene proportions.'

Moore intervened in the family squabble.

'Just leave us, then, and go back to London.'

Astrid sucked in her chest and consulted the escape map in her mind.

'If I go, Jagger and his men will come in here, and you won't be able to stop them.' She stared at Kate. 'They'll take the girl and punish the rest of you.'

Defiance flowed from Moore. 'We've got June's gun. That will stop them.'

Astrid shook her head. 'No, it won't. The only hope you have is by trusting me. I promise I won't let you down.'

The fifteen minutes are up. This is my last chance. Our last chance.

As the older women seethed, Kate stood.

'I trust you.'

The kid had a fire in her eyes and Astrid hoped she wouldn't let her down.

'Come with me then.'

Astrid watched Moore pull Courtney back before she lunged at her. Astrid retrieved the gun and the teenager followed her out. They stepped into the other house with Astrid unsure of what to tell the girl.

Kate spoke first. 'What will it be like, living with him?'

Astrid stopped her at the exit. Through the doorway, she saw Jagger and his goons waiting for them.

'How much time did you spend with him before you were rescued?'

'Only a couple of days. I knew straight away there was something wrong with him. I've seen men look at me like that before.'

'Did he hurt you?'

'No. He didn't touch me before June got me out.'

Astrid took a deep breath and hugged the girl for thirty seconds. Then she let go.

'Have these women here helped you?'

Kate nodded. 'Yes.'

'That's great. Now take my hand.'

29 ASTRID'S DILEMMA

Astrid led Kate outside as Jagger and two goons got out of the car. She saw a driver inside it, but that was it. Unfortunately, the hired help carried pistols in their hands.

She leant in close to the girl. 'Don't worry. I won't let them hurt you.'

Jagger's teeth sparkled against the moonlight, a gun in his hand.

'I thought we might have to burn you out.' He waved the weapon at her. 'Come here so my men can search you. Any surprises and I'll put a bullet in the girl's knee.'

Kate touched her throat as Astrid stepped forward.

'Anything for a thrill, eh, Paul?'

He ignored that and told his goons to frisk her.

'Don't struggle, Snow – you might like it.'

She let the two gorillas paw her, keeping a careful watch on Jagger's nervous trigger finger. When they finished, they shoved her back towards Kate.

Astrid dusted herself down. 'Paul, are you that obsessed with teenage girls you have to drive all the way up here?'

The glint in his eye turned to anger in an instant.

'People can't steal what's mine and not face the consequences and be made an example. So tell that lying bitch of a copper to come out here, or my men will shoot you and the girl.'

Astrid moved close to Kate and put her arm around the girl's back.

'You promised you wouldn't hurt anyone else.'

He smirked like a clown. 'Coppers don't count as people, especially when they've lied and spied on you.' He turned his free hand into a fist. 'I nearly had the pig as well, but she squirmed away like a stinking slug. We'd have had some fun with her then, but me and the boys will make up for it now.' He kept waving the pistol around as if he was playing the maracas in some dodgy rock and roll band until he stopped moving and pointed it at the house. 'I'm betting there are plenty of other women in there, right? And kids.' He grinned at Astrid. 'The girl and the copper, that's all I want.'

Astrid watched him return the gun to her position. 'Or else?'

'What do you think, Snow? We'll kill everyone here.'

'You'd murder a police officer and a group of women and children just for one girl?'

Jagger shrugged. 'Worse things have been done for less. One last chance before my guys start popping.'

'Even your riches won't protect you from a crime like that, Paul. So don't be stupid.'

He moved closer to her. 'Stupid? I'm the stupid one?' He twisted his head to survey their surroundings. 'There's nobody here but us, Snow. Nobody will find you and the others once we dump the bodies into the big, wide ocean. You'll be like one of those colonies that mysteriously vanishes overnight – the vanishing Vanguard; how does that sound?'

'There must be a record of you coming here?' she said.

Jagger shook his head. 'Private charter flight, Snow. One of the many privileges of being obscenely rich is the number of people you can pay to keep silent, including coppers.'

'Is Chief Inspector Thorn on your payroll?'

He placed a hand on his chest and laughed.

'That cow? God no. She hates my guts so much, I'm sure she'd kill somebody just to put me behind bars.'

'How did you know I was here?'

His laugh made the gun tremble in his fingers.

'We followed you, Snow. Did you think it would be that hard to do?'

Lazy. Lazy. Lazy.

'So there's no way out of this?'

'No pleasant ways. Now say goodbye to the kid.'

Astrid lowered her hand from Kate's shoulder to the gun in the back of the teenager's trousers. She pulled Kate closer to her as she brought the weapon around and shot both thugs in the knees. They crumpled as Jagger froze to the spot. She let go of Kate and smashed the pistol in his face. Bone cracked and blood dripped as he dropped his gun and screamed. She kicked the weapon towards the house, happy to see Ritchie run out to grab it.

Astrid nudged the other weapons away while monitoring the driver.

Then she turned to Kate. 'Are you okay, kid?'

She had the biggest grin. 'That was great. Can you do it again?'

'Maybe some other time.' Astrid spoke to Ritchie. 'Take Kate with you and go inside. Tell Pearson to call for an ambulance. And contact the Met to send officers here.'

Ritchie clutched three pistols in her hands. 'Do you need any help here?'

Astrid craned her neck towards her. 'What do you think?'

Ritchie did as instructed while Astrid went to the car. Jagger was whimpering on the ground while his thugs writhed in the dirt. She tapped on the window with the pistol. The driver wound it down.

'Are you going to shoot me?' He looked about eighteen.

'Not unless you make me.' She glanced at the kid's boss. 'The police are on their way to ask you some questions and you better tell them the truth. Do you understand?'

She lifted the gun so he could see it.

He nodded as his lips twitched. 'They pulled their guns on you and you defended yourself.'

Astrid smiled at him. 'Good lad. Jagger's going to prison for a very long time. So make sure you don't end up there with him.'

She turned and found a spot on the wall at the front of the building. Drizzle drifted down as she waited for the authorities to arrive, keeping her focus and the gun on the millionaire and his thugs. She thought of the videos on the USB drive as she watched Jagger sobbing in the dirt.

The ambulance got there first, followed by the police two minutes later. Detective Constable Ritchie greeted them with her warrant card, but Astrid guessed Chief Inspector Thorn had already spoken to their superior officer from the looks on their faces. Jagger was on his feet by then, cuffed and read his rights as he glared at her. She ignored him and spoke to Ritchie.

'Do you have enough to convict him?' She hoped this all hadn't been for nothing.

Ritchie retrieved the weapon from Astrid and put it in her pocket.

'I know where some of the bodies are buried, and Kate knows details about his trafficking operation. Once we round his thugs up, I'm sure some will blab.'

'Why didn't you go straight to Chief Thorn when you got the girl out?'

Ritchie stared at Jagger as the Barra police escorted him into the back of a vehicle.

'Because he has people on the force and I didn't know who to trust.'

'And now?'

'What choice do I have?'

'None, I guess.' Astrid nodded at the car. 'Are you going with them to the station?'

'Sure, I wouldn't miss this for the world.'

'Do you want me to come with you?'

Ritchie shook her head. 'No. I've got everything covered. I think you need to talk to your sister.'

Astrid peered at the flashing lights around them.

'Perhaps in the morning. I need sleep right now.'

She strode past Pearson and Kate, heading straight for the room they'd given her earlier. There was no lock on the door, so she pushed a heavy chair against it. She didn't get undressed, slumping on the bed and rolling onto her back. She sent Ophelia Red a text telling her Kate was safe.

Then Astrid Snow got the best night's sleep she'd had in a long time.

30 ASTRID'S BREAKFAST

Astrid was awake, showered and dressed by nine in the morning. She felt refreshed, but was wearing the same clothes she had all week. She left the room and followed the smell of fresh bacon and burnt toast into the kitchen.

'That's just how I like it.'

Her sister stared at her. 'But not how I like it. Do you still have your eggs scrambled, Astrid?'

She sat in the chair, not used to her sister calling her by her first name.

'I'm surprised you remembered.'

Courtney poured them both a cup of coffee. 'Olivia told me.'

Astrid warmed her hands on the drink. 'Of course she did.' She studied her sister as Courtney put the food on the plate. 'Is this going to be a family reunion where we air all our grievances? We'll be here a long time if it is.'

As she considered that, Pearson and Moore entered the room.

'Are you feeling refreshed, Astrid?'

Pearson's chirpiness was less irritating than yesterday.

'Don't worry. I'll be out of your hair once I've eaten.'

'There's no rush. June's colleagues from the Met arrived in the early hours and escorted Jagger and his people back to London.' Astrid was surprised Thorn hadn't called her. 'But I was hoping you might do me another favour.'

Astrid bit through black toast and felt it stick in her teeth. 'What favour?'

Pearson took the seat next to Astrid, and Courtney gave her a coffee. There was a quick look of something between her sister and the Vanguard boss.

'Can you take Vanessa, Courtney and Olivia back to London with you?'

She nearly spat toast all over herself. 'What?'

'You convinced me to expand our enterprise.'

'I did?'

'Yes, you were right to raise concerns about people leaving Vanguard and being unprepared for the big, wide world. So I'm going to open education centres in some bigger cities, starting with London.' She glanced at Courtney. 'And your sister and Vanessa will run it.'

Astrid lost some food this time as bacon bits fell from her lips. She wiped at her mouth as she spoke to her sister.

'You're quitting teaching?'

Courtney threw oil into the frying pan as she replied.

'I'll still be teaching, plus I've got a house to return to, and Olivia misses her friends in London.'

Astrid pushed her back into the chair and wondered if she was dreaming. Then, when her sister spoke again, she knew she must be.

'It will take some time to get everything organised there, so I need you to look after Olivia for a while.'

Astrid bit into her lip and tasted blood. 'How long?'

'A couple of weeks, probably. Is that okay?'

The bacon slipped down her throat as Astrid's heart tried to jump through her chest.

Looking after a seven-year-old might prove harder than catching a serial killer.

THANK YOU!

Thank you, dear reader for purchasing this book.

If you enjoyed reading about Astrid Snow her story continues in these books:

The Astrid Snow series
Book one: Don't Fear the Reaper
Book two: The Killing Moon
Book three: Lost in America
Book four: Gone to Texas

Short Stories
Call Me: An Astrid Snow Short Story
Dark Snow: An Astrid Snow Short Story

Many thanks to my wonderful wife for all her support and patience.

Extra special thanks to Karina Gallagher for being a dedicated reader of my work.

The Final Girl edited by Alison Jack.

Cover design by James, GoOnWrite.com

OPHELIA RED

Ophelia Red first appeared in the Astrid Snow thriller, The Final Girl. Here are the initial two chapters from her first solo novel.

SHE'S IN PARTIES

The smell of rosebushes filled the air. Ophelia Red, a bee in one hand and a Coke in the other, marched through the garden. The revellers parted before her as they glanced at Ophelia's ruby hair and the insect sitting in her palm. The bee tickled her skin as she put it down, pouring Coke on her finger and offering it to the distressed creature. The bee devoured it in a heartbeat.

'You'll kill it like that.'

She peered at the man in swimming trunks staring at her. A lion tattoo covered his chest as the sunlight reflected off his gold tooth. She couldn't see the skin on his arms or legs, only tattoos of mythical creatures: dragons, unicorns and elves.

'What?' she said.

He shook his head, sending dandruff into the roses.

'You want a solution of sugar and water to restore an exhausted bee, and only offer it white granulated sugar. Any artificial or diet sweeteners can harm them, and that Coke will kill it.'

As he spoke, the bee fluttered into life and flew away.

Ophelia grinned at the illustrated man. 'It was that or a shot of vodka, and we don't want a drunken bee terrorising the guests at this shindig, do we?'

He came at her like a vulture at a corpse, smelling of sweat and cheap cologne.

'Did you know the first Coke drink was red wine mixed with cocaine, advertised as a brain tonic to relieve headaches and exhaustion?'

She didn't encourage him with a reply, knowing it would have been like buying Jeffrey Dahmer a second fridge. Instead, she returned to the kitchen and grabbed a bottle of Mexican lager. From the living room, Madonna was singing *Like A Virgin*. Ophelia took a long swig and buried the memories of her father's alcoholism behind those of her mother's indifference.

'I bet there's few of them here.' She turned to see a purple-haired woman grinning at her. 'Virgins, I mean.'

The alcohol warmed Ophelia's mouth. 'Is this a sex party?'

The newcomer spat vodka over the floor. 'Good God, I hope not.' She glanced into the living room before peering through the window into the garden. 'Have you seen the state of the men here?'

Ophelia slurped her drink. 'I don't know anyone here. I'm a gate crasher.'

The purple-haired woman didn't seem to care.

'My boss asked me to come with him. He feels it's easier to meet women if you're already with one. Like being married is attractive to women, you know?' Ophelia didn't know. 'He thinks it proves something about him if at least one woman already deems him dateable.'

'What do you do?' Ophelia said.

'My name's Chloe and I'm a funeral director.'

That's appropriate.

'You must have some tales to tell.'

She grabbed Ophelia and pulled her towards the window.

'You don't know the half of it.' She pointed at the clown in the garden entertaining the guests. 'Do you see that bloke?'

'Ronald McDonald?'

Chloe narrowed her eyes in confusion. 'No, that comedian over there. We had a dead clown at the funeral parlour once, buried in a full costume with makeup. The whole family was clowns, and all the friends were clowns. And at the family's request, the funeral directors were clowns too. They supplied costumes and did our makeup. Family and friends had one tear drop painted near the eye.'

Ophelia sipped on the drink, her interest now awakened. 'Doesn't it bother you, staring into so many dead faces?'

It had never bothered her, but she was curious how others felt.

Chloe's face brightened. 'No, never. The eyes usually flatten after death like an old grape. They do, however, remain with the body. We don't remove them. Instead, you can use an eye cap to put over the flattened eyeball to recreate the natural curvature. You can inject tissue builder directly into the eyeball and fill it up. And sometimes, the embalming fluid will fill the eye to normal size.'

'It sounds fascinating.'

Chloe beamed. 'Well, I think so, but most people don't.' She leant closer so Ophelia could smell the lavender in her hair. 'Many people don't understand. I've lost several boyfriends because of it and my mother thinks I'm a vampire.'

'At least the customers don't talk back to you.'

Chloe snorted like an asthmatic hyena. 'That's true.'

'What made you go into that line of work?'

'Childhood trauma.' She laughed again. 'No, not really. When I was ten, there was a terrible collision near my house, and a man in a truck didn't make it. When the coroner arrived, my family and I stood around with the neighbours. He pronounced him deceased. Then they put him on a stretcher and his head turned to the side, looking straight at me. I remember being curious about what happens to the human body when people die.'

Ophelia knew what she meant. She was twelve years old when she realised something was different with her, sitting cross-legged and ankle-deep in blood that wasn't hers, reciting the alphabet backwards.

'Are you still curious?'

Chloe nodded. 'The human brain is fascinating, especially when you hold one in your hands.' She inched closer to Ophelia. 'But that's enough about me. So what do you do, mysterious party crasher?'

Ophelia should have told her something mundane, a fictitious job that wouldn't leave any lasting memories for when the police arrived. But the boredom had got the better of her, and now she wanted some fun.

And maybe she'd drunk too much.

'I'm an online dating ghost-writer.'

Confusion crept across Chloe's face. 'You set up dates for ghosts?'

Ophelia laughed. 'No. I write profiles for online dating sites for those who struggle to produce their own.'

'Wow,' Chloe said. 'Isn't that like lying?'

'Of course not. I'm cupid with a computer, that's all.'

Chloe pointed out of the window. 'Maybe you could

write one for that loser.' Ophelia peered at the tattooed man standing on his hands. 'Duff by name and by nature.'

'That's Larry Duff?'

'Yes. Do you know him?'

Ophelia shook her head. 'I overheard somebody talking about him. Isn't this his house?' Now she had confirmation on the target.

Chloe frowned. 'It's his celebration. This is in poor taste if you ask me.'

'Why?'

Chloe lowered her voice. 'He hit a ten-year-old girl with his car, killing her. You'd think he'd go to prison for that, wouldn't you?' Ophelia nodded. 'All he got was a six-month driving ban and points on his licence. It's scandalous.'

Ophelia agreed. 'The girl's family must be devastated.'

'Oh, it got even worse for them. The father jumped off a bridge not long after his daughter's death, and from what I've heard, the mother is now sucking on sleeping tablets as if they're sweets. She can't pay the mortgage on the house, so she'll also lose that.' She nodded at Duff amusing his guests. 'And all because that moron was on his phone while driving.'

'Did he tell the police that?'

Chloe whispered, 'Nope. Only his friends know about it.'

Ophelia peered at the illustrated man, now knowing why somebody had hired her to kill him. She rarely knew the reasons for her contracts, but she only had two rules: no kids and nothing within thirty miles of her home. Two days ago, she'd arrived in Leeds – seventy-five miles from her place in Redcar – spending the first day scouting the area around Duff's house. So when she'd turned up in the street this afternoon, it had been a pleasant surprise to see the celebrations, surveying the premises as she hid in plain sight amongst revellers.

She hadn't planned to kill Duff there and then, but she had the means in her bag if she had the right opening: fast and slow-acting poisons; two syringes; a small knife; and a garrotte. Ophelia thought about those tools as she heard *Dancing Queen* blasting through the house. She left Chloe in the kitchen and returned to the garden, watching as Duff hugged a clown. She sat in a chair near the roses, reaching into her jacket to remove one of her phones. She pushed her thumb into the screen to unlock it and opened the app for her Cayman Islands bank account, smiling when she saw the deposit for half of her payment. Then she returned the phone to her pocket. Now it was a waiting game.

OPHELIA STAYED INSIDE until ten o'clock, watching everybody leave apart from her and four others. Before exiting the front door, she checked the garden and every room. Then she went across the road and waited some more. By midnight, everyone but Duff had left the building. She gave it another twenty minutes before moving to the rear of the house and the garden, gripping the key she'd taken earlier. She let herself in and peered into her bag, unsure what to use to kill him. She moved into the living room and considered the options, finding him slumped on the sofa. He was drunk and out cold.

Time for an old favourite.

She returned to the kitchen for a tea towel. She had to place the cloth over his mouth, her knee on his stomach, and nature and the alcohol would do the rest. The pressure would induce him to vomit, and since it wouldn't have anywhere to go because of the towel, he'd choke. Ophelia was moving towards him when she heard the front door open.

Shit!

She hurried into the far corner behind a large bookshelf.

Maybe I should sit on the sofa and pretend I'm drunk from the party.

Before she could do anything, a blonde woman entered the room, pointing a gun at the sleeping Larry Duff.

Her hand trembled as she spoke. 'This is for killing my daughter, you piece of shit.'

Daughter? The girl he'd killed – this was the mother?

Ophelia could let her shoot him and still get paid.

But if she's here to kill him, she can't have been the one who hired me.

The woman was caressing the trigger as Ophelia stepped out of the shadows.

'You don't need to do that.'

She jerked her head towards Ophelia, swinging the pistol around.

'What... what did you say?'

Ophelia kept a careful eye on that weapon. 'What's your daughter's name?'

A single tear dripped onto the woman's cheek. 'Laura. Her name was Laura.' She glanced at Duff. 'And this piece of shit killed her. The law did nothing, and he's here partying like a fucking rock star.'

'How did you get into the house?'

'The front door was unlocked.'

Great. I should have checked that.

She stepped closer to Ophelia. 'Are you his girlfriend?'

Ophelia shook her head. 'No. I'm here to kill him.'

The woman's eyes glazed over. 'Why? Did he hurt you as well?'

'Does it matter why? You can leave and I'll ensure he gets what's coming to him.'

She waved the gun at Ophelia. 'It matters to me. And why should I believe you? You could be his partner and a lying scumbag like he is.'

'Do you want to watch me do it?'

The woman thought about it for ten seconds. 'Yes.'

Ophelia moved towards Duff, watching his chest move up and down as the drool slipped between his lips. The lion tattoo glared at her, growling as Duff's ribs vibrated. She climbed onto the sofa, her legs on either side of him, glancing at the distraught mother.

'What's your name?'

'Katrina,' she said.

'Last chance to leave, Katrina.'

She shook her head and the gun. 'No. I need to see this.'

Ophelia placed the material over his face, and then put her knee on his stomach. After thirty seconds, his eyes flicked open in panic. She bathed in his fear as he tried to fight her, but he was out of luck. It took four minutes before he stopped struggling and she got off him, hanging onto the vomit-stained cloth.

Katrina walked to him, gazing into the dead face of the man who'd killed her daughter. 'What do we do now?'

Ophelia took the gun from her, putting it into her pocket along with the cloth.

'Did you drive here?'

Katrina nodded. 'Yes, but I didn't park near the house. It's a ten-minute walk from here.'

Ophelia grabbed her arm and pulled her into the kitchen.

'We're leaving through the back. Stick to the shadows and twenty yards in front of me, and head straight for the car.'

Katrina didn't argue. Ophelia followed her into the street.

Now, what do I do with her?

BACK TO THE OLD HOUSE

'You smell of vomit,' Katrina said.

They were sitting in her car, and Ophelia thought the grieving mother might be about to throw up.

'Do you have alcohol at home?'

Katrina nodded. 'Plenty.'

Ophelia fastened the seatbelt. 'Okay. Take us there. We've got a lot to talk about.'

THIRTY MINUTES LATER, she sat in the living room, sipping on a gin and tonic. They'd taken a detour to dispose of the gun and the vomit cloth in the river. Now Katrina slumped on the sofa opposite her.

'Why did you kill Duff?'

Ophelia chewed on a piece of ice. 'Somebody paid me.'

Katrina's eyes bulged. 'Who would do that?'

Ophelia shrugged. 'I thought it might be you.'

'Me?' Katrina laughed. 'I can barely pay for food. How much does a murder cost?'

'It varies. Duff was worth fifty grand to someone.'

Katrina grabbed at her throat before she choked on her whisky.

'Fifty grand! Jesus.'

Ophelia swallowed the ice. 'It's a decent living.'

'Do you normally leave witnesses?'

The cube chilled her mouth. 'No.'

'So you brought me here to kill me?'

'I'm not sure what I'll do with you.' Ophelia glanced around the living room, seeing toys and children's books everywhere. 'Do you have any suggestions?'

Katrina's face darkened. Reaching for the bottle on the table next to her, she held it so Ophelia could see the contents: sleeping pills.

'You'll be quicker than these, and do me a favour.' Her eyelids trembled like butterfly wings on fast forward. 'I can't pay you, but I don't want the vomit thing either. Do you have a quick and painless option?'

A chill ran through Ophelia's fingers. 'What do you do for a living?'

Katrina returned the pills to the table. 'I trained as a computer programmer at university. That's where I met Brian. Now, I'm a forensic computer analyst. My husband and I worked for the same company before things got complicated.'

Ophelia scrutinised her, understanding she wasn't talking about her daughter's death.

'What happened?'

'It wasn't computers that brought Brian and me together, but our love of gambling. It started at university. They had several quiz machines in the bar, and we'd spend hours on them. Unfortunately, it didn't help with either of our student debts. By the time we got our degrees, we owed over a hundred grand between us.'

'How long ago was this?'

'Ten years. I was pregnant with Laura. Once we left university, we lived with his parents before finding jobs for the same company. His mother hated me, but I put up with it. Then we married, bought a house, and had a lovely baby girl to fawn over.'

'Had you started paying your debt?'

'Hardly. What we owed never seemed to reduce, with the mortgage payments, childcare expenses, and everyday bills.'

'But you had well-paid jobs?'

'Until six months ago, just before Laura's death.'

'You were both still betting?'

Katrina removed a phone from her pocket and placed it on her leg.

'Do you know how easy it is to place a bet online?' Ophelia shook her head. 'Gambling is like having a frontal lobotomy. You sit there and listen to the music, which relaxes you and makes you feel better.' She waved the mobile at Ophelia. 'And when it's all done electronically, so you don't even have the money in your hand, it's like living in a fairy tale. All of it is unreal, and you have flashing lights and music attacking your senses. So it doesn't matter what you lose because none of it is real.'

'How much do you and your husband owe?'

'Including our student debts, about a hundred grand. And we're six months behind on the mortgage for this house. We talked about going to a loan shark, but...'

'You stole from your company instead?'

'It was easier that way. We both had access to the finances through the computer system.' She lowered her head. 'But we weren't very good at covering our tracks. Our employer discovered what we'd done less than a week into our criminal careers. We were both sacked on the spot. I thought that was the worst thing that could happen to me, but it wasn't.' She raised her eyes to stare at Ophelia. 'A few days later, Duff hits Laura with his car. And then Brian jumps off a bridge.' She finished her drink. 'So here we are, and you're about to do me a favour.'

Ophelia cradled the glass in her hands. 'Perhaps.'

'How did you become an assassin for hire?'

'It's a long story.'

'I've got plenty of time. Or have I?' Her laugh rattled the top of the table between them. 'How do your clients contact you?'

'Through the dark web.'

Katrina put her drink down. 'But how do you know you can trust them?'

Ophelia relaxed on the sofa.

Why am I talking to her like this? Is it because I'm going to kill her, anyway?

I can't leave any witnesses.

And this woman wants to die – she's got nothing left to live for.

'They pay half the fee upfront, the minimum being twenty-five thousand non- refundable. So nobody is going to throw that amount away on a whim.'

'Yes, but what if it's the police or somebody else trying to trap you?'

Ophelia shrugged. 'That's one of the risks you take in this business. Once I've received the payment and the details, I check the target to ensure the contract is legit.'

'And that's what you did with Duff?'

'Yes.'

'And you thought it was me who'd hired you?'

'I didn't know and didn't care. I don't look to see who is hiring me or ask why. I just do the job.'

'What if you feel uneasy about the contract? Say if it's an innocent person or a child?'

'I don't kill children, and nobody is innocent.'

'What if a client pays you to kill someone doing good in the world?'

'I don't make moral judgements.'

Katrina laughed. 'Maybe you could teach me how to do it. I could pay my debts then.'

'You believe you're capable of killing a person?'

'Yes. I would have killed Duff.'

'You had good reason for that. But think about those innocent people you asked me about. Could you kill one of them?'

Katrina grabbed her empty glass and stood. 'While I muse on that, would you like another drink?'

Ophelia got up. 'Sure, but I need the bathroom first.'

'Top of the stairs, second on your left.'

She headed for the kitchen while Ophelia went to the toilet. Once Ophelia had finished, she checked the bedrooms, stepping into one that must have been Laura's: everything was purple, including the wallpaper and the sheets. She glanced at the computer desk and the full bookcase, recognising novels she'd loved as a kid: the *His Dark Materials* trilogy; *The Dark is Rising*; *Earthsea*; and *The Arcane* series. She peered at the covers and remembered the collection of books and comics she'd had as a teenager. They'd been her only friends until the day her mother had tossed them away.

'You're too old for childish things,' her mother had said as she ripped out the pages of eight-year-old Ophelia's cherished copy of *The Golden Compass*.

But that was long ago, and Ophelia had a different name then. She pushed the memory back into the shadows and wondered what to do with the woman downstairs.

Katrina has nothing to live for, so I'll be doing her a favour.

As she considered that, she heard glass breaking below. She left Laura's bedroom and returned to the living room.

Only to find a masked man with a large knife placed against Katrina's neck.

'Which one of you is Rossetti?' he said.

Ophelia scanned the room, checking for other intruders, unsurprised that he knew her secret name.

'Are you from Hitsville?'

He pushed the blade closer to Katrina's flesh. 'I guess it's you, then. Get on your knees and put your hands behind you.'

She shook her head. 'No.'

'Do it,' he growled. 'Or I'll slit her throat.'

Ophelia laughed. 'I don't care. She means nothing to me.' She stepped towards him. 'What's your name in Hitsville?'

He moved back and pushed up against the sofa with Katrina against him.

'I'm not telling you that. Now get on your knees.'

Ophelia gazed into Katrina's eyes. Then she nodded to the grieving mother. Katrina grinned as she stamped on her assailant's foot. He screamed as she wriggled from his grasp, the knife brushing against her throat and drawing blood. She fell forward and Ophelia grabbed her, the two women stumbling back as the masked man jumped on one leg. When he lowered the blade, Ophelia pounced.

She threw herself into him, taking them over the sofa

and into a table. Photos of Laura and Katrina shattered on the floor, showering glass and cutting her fingers. She grabbed for the knife with her other hand, clawing at his wrist as he tried to push her away.

But she failed, and he dropped the blade.

He got both hands around her neck and squeezed.

Ophelia's breath fizzed from her as she clutched at his arms. They were stuck in the space between the back of the sofa and the wall, her body twitching as his nails dug into her skin. She pulled at his clothes, trying to drag him away. Ophelia peered into the eyes behind the mask, hearing him grunt as he squeezed harder.

Her eyelids flickered, and her vision blurred as a porcelain figure of a pig crashed into his head. It split into pieces, raining blood everywhere, forcing him to let go of her and jerk towards his attacker.

It was the opportunity Ophelia needed.

As she coughed, she raised her arm and punched him in the gut. Then she grabbed his waist and threw him into the wall, so he hit it head first. She wiped her throat and staggered towards him, unable to stop Katrina from plunging the knife into his chest. He groaned as he clutched at the blade, slipping down onto the carpet.

Ophelia rested against the sofa and watched the blood seep through his clothes. Then she removed his mask.

'Do you recognise him?' Katrina said.

'Nope.' Ophelia gazed at the dying man. 'What's your Hitsville name?'

Blood dripped over his lips. 'Darknight64,' he spluttered.

'Did you follow us from Duff's house?'

The word crawled out of his mouth. 'Yes.'

'How much did they pay you for me?'

'A lot.'

Then he died.

Ophelia turned from him. She went to the kitchen and poured a gin and tonic. When she returned to the living room, Katrina was on the sofa, supping straight from the whisky bottle and rubbing at the wound on her neck. Ophelia sat opposite her.

'What's Hitsville?' Katrina said.

The liquid scratched at Ophelia's throat. 'It's the corner of the dark web where assassins ply their trade.'

'And you're Rossetti?'

'You can call me Ophelia.'

'Okay. Why would another assassin try to kill you?'

'I don't know, but he followed us from Duff's place without knowing which of us was the target.'

'But he would have killed us both?'

'Yes. You can't leave witnesses.' She stared at Katrina. 'But he had to make sure before doing the deed.' She smiled at her. 'Do you still want to kill people for money?'

Katrina glanced at the corpse in the corner. 'Well, I've already started with a freebie.'

Ophelia finished her drink. 'Indeed.'

'What do we do now?'

'We?' Ophelia stood. 'I don't have to do anything. You're the one with the dead man in your house.'

She went to the body, checking for anything that might illuminate the situation. Katrina followed her.

'You're going to leave me like this after I saved your life?'

Ophelia found nothing on the man. 'I had everything under control before you interfered.'

Katrina laughed. 'You were lulling him in by letting him strangle you, then?'

Ophelia glanced at the damage in the room before returning her gaze to the woman who'd killed the mysterious assassin.

What am I going to do now?

ABOUT THE AUTHOR

Andrew French lives amongst faded seaside glamour on the North East coast of England. He likes gin and cats but not together, new music and old movies, curry and ice cream. Slow bike rides and long walks to the pub are his usual exercise, as well as flicking through the pages of good books and the memoirs of bad people.

Find out more at www.andrewsfrench.com

Facebook:

https://www.facebook.com/A-S-French-Author-150145625006018

Twitter:

www.twitter.com/andrewfrench100

Instagram:

www.instagram.com/andrewfrench100

And replies to all his email at mail@andrewsfrench.com

If you have the time, please leave a review at Amazon or Goodreads

Thank you!